THE ANCIENT HOURS

ALSO BY MICHAEL BIBLE

Empire of Light

Sophia

Cowboy Maloney's Electric City

Simple Machines

My Second Best Bear Rug

Gorilla Math

~ THE ~

ANCIENT
HOURS

◆

MICHAEL

BIBLE

⌂ MELVILLE HOUSE

BROOKLYN
LONDON

Melville House Publishing
46 John Street
Brooklyn, NY 11201
and
Melville House UK
Suite 2000
16/18 Woodford Road
London E7 0HA

mhpbooks.com
@melvillehouse

ISBN: 978-1-61219-864-4
ISBN: 978-1-61219-865-1 (eBook)

Library of Congress Control Number: 2020944084

Designed by Richard Oriolo

Printed in the United States of America

1 3 5 7 9 10 8 6 4 2

A catalog record for this book is available from the Library of Congress

THE ANCIENT HOURS

HARMONY

2018

1

WE WERE INNOCENT. Believed we were special. Drunk every weekend at the mall. The world was in our hands. Time didn't matter. Love was a given. Death was afraid of us. Now we've got gray in our beards. The sky bruises purple. The mall is dead. We're the old men we promised we'd never become. Spending our days in the corner booth at the Starlight Diner arguing life's vagaries. Our town, Harmony, is typical. Just like yours. Full of saints and sinners you can't tell apart.

On late summer Sunday afternoons the light spills over the old clock tower and projects a shadow on the square as big as a mountain. The florist, Floyd Williams, lines his windows with orange gladiolus the size of antique sabers. He has a scar from a fistfight with his youngest son that started over his drinking. Ben White helps Sue Meadows from her car so she can get her back pills. He's sleeping with a man in Greensboro that his wife doesn't know about. The fiddle shop is opening. Doug Lightfoot is helping Mary Beth Taylor get her tuning just right. Last year Doug got Mary Beth pregnant even though he's twice her age. Drove her to Charlotte to get it taken care of. Bud Rogers, the football coach, picks up his car from the body shop. Has a long talk with Theo Knight about the Panthers' chances this year. Bud sells a little weed on the side mostly to kids from Harmony High School. Theo spends his evenings weeping about his wife who went missing ten years ago.

We found an old picture from our eighth-grade class trip to city hall. Iggy stands apart from the group. A bright October day. Orange leaves fall down behind us. Mrs. Maple's red hair up in a bun. Most of us wear school hoodies except for Iggy. We've tried to understand why he wore a yellow rain jacket on a sunny day. Was it a sign? We studied his face for something, anything, that might show us what he would become. That trip to city hall was supposed to teach us about the history of Harmony. We took a bus downtown from school that morning. Ate ham sandwiches and green apples for lunch.

Harmony is older than America, Mayor Presley told us. He was a fat, bald man with a tightly trimmed beard. A lifelong bachelor, his family had been in Harmony for over a century. Raised sheepdogs as a hobby. When you drove by his house late at night the blue light from the TV was always on.

As we toured city hall, Mayor Presley told us the story of how German and Scots-Irish from Pennsylvania began to settle in this part of North Carolina as early as 1753. They grew crops in the fertile soil with fresh water from the Bluebird River. There was a log cabin that housed worship on Sunday and would one day become the site of the First Baptist Church of Harmony. In 1850 a brick factory arrived founded by JC Pearl that still operates to this day.

At the end of the tour we sat in a semicircle around Mayor Presley in his office with the giant town seal above him. A few of his dogs lay at his feet.

Maybe you could tell the students about our economy, Mrs. Maple said.

Of course, he said. Harmony is one of the largest producers of tobacco in the foothills.

We remember the next part clearly. Mayor Presley went into his drawer and pulled out a leaf of dried Carolina tobacco and passed it around and we smelled it and passed it on. It was light brown and fragile. When it came to Iggy he took out a Zippo lighter and lit it on fire. Mrs. Maple blew it out. She grabbed him by the arm and they went into the hall. Mr. Presley looked at the half-burned leaf and opened a window.

Now boys and girls, he said. I want you to go around the room and promise me that you will never smoke.

We all promised except for Amanda Armstrong. She started crying.

I won't, she said. I won't promise.

Smoking's so bad for you, Mr. Presley said.

My daddy's a farmer, she said. If everybody quits we'll go broke.

We looked to Mr. Presley to see what he had to say about that. He smiled.

There are plenty of smokers in China, he said.

Won't the Chinese get cancer, too, Amanda asked.

Mr. Presley laughed.

I'm only worried about the boys and girls here in Harmony, he said. I'm not the mayor of China.

Just then Mrs. Maple came back in with Iggy.

I'm sorry I burned up your leaf, he said.

That's OK, Mr. Presley said. I forgive you as long as you promise you'll never start smoking.

Iggy looked at the ground and nodded.

I plan on quitting soon, he said.

Ms. Rivers still works here at the Starlight as she did back then when we'd smoke Camel Lights by the pack after a high school football game. Some of us had crushes on her, she was only a few years our senior. But now she's old like us. Still here. Stuck in this town. As she refills our coffee, talk returns to Iggy as it so often does on afternoons like these. Someone re-tells the story of the incident when we were kids back in the nineties. The summer before our freshman year. Iggy was al-ways part of our group until then. We'd all gotten onto sports teams or started bands and Iggy was still playing chess by himself and taking piano lessons. One of us, we don't remem-ber who, came up with the nickname "Cheese Grits." We'd de-cided that Iggy was cheesy and the name seemed to fit. When we'd call his house his mom always said he wasn't around. We figured he was up in his room hiding. Late that summer we got into someone's dad's whiskey collection and at midnight went out in the neighborhood to pull pranks. We rolled the Spencers' house and dumped all the outdoor furniture into Dr. Johnson's pool. We raided the Mumfords' garden and took huge bell pep-pers to Iggy's house. We left them on his front porch with a note. Looking back we don't remember why we thought it would be funny to do this, except that we were teenagers and drunk. The note said we'd kidnapped Iggy and if they didn't give us one thousand dollars they'd never see him again. Throughout the next afternoon, still hungover, each of us got a knock on the door from Iggy's parents. Iggy's mom wore no makeup as if she'd been crying all morning and his father was dressed to work in the yard. They told us that all summer Iggy had been saving up money from mowing lawns. He'd taken his cash downtown to buy a video game but on the way there he was assaulted. His money was stolen and he was left for dead in an alley. He was in the hospital for a week and had been at home recovering for months. What we didn't know, couldn't have known, was that morning when his parents found the note, Iggy had gone out for the first time since he was beaten up. They thought the attackers had kidnapped him. Finally, to their relief, he walked through the door hours later. Iggy told them he thought he knew who'd done it. As his parents sat with us in our kitchens and living rooms, we admitted it was us. Told them it was supposed to be a joke. That we had no idea about the attack. Our parents made us write letters to Iggy telling him we were sorry, but who knows if he read them or not. After that we tried to call him a few times to hang out, put the whole thing behind us, but he never talked to us again. We'd mainly put him out of our minds after that. He became a character in stories from our youth even though we sometimes still saw him around school. Heard rumors about him and his friends Paul and Cleo. We lived separate from him and believed, naively, that he too was having a normal high school experience full of keg parties and weekends at the lake. Perhaps he was, but we didn't really think of him again until after graduation and that morning at the First Baptist Church.

The fire was already out when the news trucks arrived. The governor came shortly after. Then senators and congresspeople and finally the president, too. They made speeches. Made promises. Raised money to rebuild. Then the president left and the governor left and the congresspeople left and the news people packed up for some new tragedy. For days an eerie silence filled the town. No one knew exactly what to do. Some of us from Iggy's graduating class gathered to discuss things in a corner booth at the Starlight Diner. That was eighteen years ago.

Some have called him a monster, a terrorist, a psychopath, but he was also just a kid. We've found it impossible to reconcile those facts. In the intervening years we've questioned why Iggy had such disregard for life. Each of us lost something that day and the grief still haunts us. But what was most damaging was our ignorance, our inability to conceive of such brutality. A privileged existence that protected us from seeing the true nature of things. We've tried to piece back together time itself, to find some way to undo it.

Tragedy tends to follow similar trajectories. A pattern we're now all too familiar with. The horror of the incident. Brief hours of confusion and grief, followed by days of anger. Weeks of outrage. Some blame violence in movies or video games. Some blame mental illness. Thoughts and prayers and thoughts and prayers and thoughts and prayers. Raise some money. Change is now. Marches and petitions and speeches. Then nothing. Then more nothing.

We could talk all night, but Ms. Rivers is kicking us out.

You know the bars are open late, she says.

We don't like the bars, we say. Full of young folks.

We tip her well and as we leave there is one last memory from that eighth-grade trip. Later that day we toured the county jail with the sheriff. Mrs. Maple joked that he would come arrest all us kids if we talked in class.

Which one of these kids is your worst, the sheriff asked.

Mrs. Maple looked us over and smiled. She pointed at Amanda Armstrong. She was wearing pigtails with bows.

I can't arrest such a pretty girl, he said. How 'bout this little troublemaker?

He grabbed Iggy and put him against the wall and hand-cuffed him. We howled with laughter. Iggy was kind of smiling too at first. It was all in good fun. Then the sheriff put him in a cell and locked it. We thought that was even funnier and we all laughed harder. The sheriff escorted us out of the room and left Iggy in there for a minute alone. The look on his face when we returned. We'll never forget it.

2

ANOTHER NIGHT AT the Starlight Diner and Ms. Rivers takes our orders. The horizon is a black sliver against the sun. All our old mysteries unite. Our coffees get cold. We call our wives and tell them not to wait up. We present our latest research to the group. Harmony had a much darker history than the one we were told. On that eighth-grade trip Mayor Presley left out the Molasses Massacre. We found that there were many other stories the town fathers wished to remain forgotten.

In 1843, the Jones brothers (half-black, half-Cherokee) accidently spilled a barrel of molasses on a prominent lawyer, Don Sherill. Although Sherill forgave the brothers at the time, he recounted the incident later at a barbershop in town. A drunken mob formed among the patrons and they tried to take the Jones brothers from their home. They were injured in the melee but survived. They threatened to take Sherill and others to court. It was forbidden for a person of color to take a white man to court at the time, but even the thought of it enraged the citizenry. They formed a mob and hanged the two brothers on the oak tree in the very spot where our picture was taken outside city hall. Mayor Presley didn't tell us that once freed from slavery, black residents of Harmony formed a neighborhood on the south side called Yellow Hill. In 1867, a blacksmith named M. Horice Warner was found to be picnicking on the hillside with a six-year-old girl and was accused of sexually assaulting her. He was taken from his home by a mob of hundreds and dragged by horses through the streets of Yellow Hill. Later people claimed the man was a friend of the girl's father and the interaction was innocent.

The night goes on. Ms. Rivers lets us stay longer while she cleans up. Someone at the table brings up Iggy's friend Johnny Nightshade. How his mother, Trudy, was fired from teaching in the public schools for praying in the classroom.

There's a new court order that forbids it, the new principal, Doug Shepard said.

So what, Trudy said.

It's from the Supreme Court, he said.

Principal Shepard was a tiny bow-tied man and liked to tell anyone who would listen how he graduated from Duke University with honors.

The Supreme Court is not the supreme being, Trudy said.

The story goes she knelt in his office and prayed out loud that the sinners in the Harmony public schools would not suffer long in the fires of hell—and then walked out. That Sunday, Pastor Green told the story in his sermon at First Baptist. Mrs. Gregory, the jeweler's wife, put up funds to build a Christian academy downtown that fall. Trudy was their first hire.

For those who don't want their children to be raised in a godless Marxist indoctrination factory, Trudy said.

Despite her cantankerous nature, reports from her classes at Harmony Christian Academy were generally positive. She could be a kind, sensitive teacher and in certain moods had enormous patience for her students. In class she was known for reciting long poems and monologues. She was so good at it that on the first day of school when she'd launch into Shakespeare students would turn around to see if she was reading it off the back wall. She taught many of our parents the classics. Some of our older siblings still remember her classes in the later years when she'd stopped making sense. She would mix her own biography with that of the characters in famous novels. It was like time had worked on her in a way we could never understand. As if the books she read were a series of misremembered tales and she was their heroine.

She was virulently antigay, not unheard of in the South in those days, but Trudy was over-the-top even then. Some of us suspected perhaps her husband was having an affair with Mayor Presley. They sang in the church choir and took cruises together. In her later teaching years, when progressive thinking was a bit less rare in Harmony, Trudy's students would ask her about Truman Capote or Walt Whitman or Oscar Wilde. She would immediately launch into "Sinners in the Hands of an Angry God."

After her husband died and she retired, she would ride to town on his motorcycle, a little Jack Russell in the sidecar. There was an unconfirmed rumor she'd been a stunt pilot's girl in Arkansas as a teenager. Some kind of barnstorming show where she was strapped half-naked standing on top of the wing as the plane did loops and dives. Allegedly there were pictures.

Above all, through the years, she loved her son. Johnny was her only boy and our parents told us he was exactly the same when they were growing up together. Calling himself Johnny Nightshade even then. Same cabbie hat and soul patch. Carried his saxophone everywhere. They said during middle school he tried not to talk for a full week. Only used his sax to speak. It was funny at first, they said, but after a while it got super annoying. Honking all day like a goose through the halls.

As a mother of a child prodigy, Trudy would often say unironically.

When Johnny failed to gain admission to any of the famous music conservatories, she blamed the admissions people.

They held his love of Jesus against him, she told Ms. Rivers at the Starlight Diner one night. It's better if Johnny stays right here with me.

And then there was the business of Iggy and Johnny playing music together. Of course there were whispers. A man as old as Johnny palling around with someone as young as Iggy. Trudy testified at Iggy's trial about their relationship:

Johnny had all sorts of friends throughout the years. He was quite popular socially. And this boy Iggy, he was, well, kindly, lost. My Johnny gave the boy something to live for and the gift of music. Iggy was quiet, I remember that. I could barely hear him. Almost whispered when he talked. Johnny brought him home one night and I said this one needs to project his voice. The theater would be good for him.

When Iggy went away to the wilderness school, Trudy

would write him and send care packages. She threw a dinner in his honor at the Starlight Diner when he came back to Harmony. In the months leading up to the incident, Trudy saw Iggy almost weekly at church. Johnny was starting a new modern music ministry at the time and they would stay late during rehearsals.

At trial Trudy was asked point blank if Johnny was homosexual. She said she would not dignify the question with a response.

I'm devoted to the First Baptist Church, she said. Christian women don't speak of such things.

Members of the church said she was the first one in the sanctuary on Sunday and the last to leave. She always brought fresh flowers from her garden. During the Great Depression her grandmother started a flower shop downtown that sold only gladiolus because she could get cheap bulbs from a catalogue. When someone was sick in the congregation she was the first to visit and bring food. Same when one of the church members passed away. She never said the word *died*, she always said *passed away*.

There's an upper room waiting for us, she'd say. Those willing to take Christ's love into their hearts.

Trudy almost didn't go to church the Sunday of the incident. She'd been fighting off a bad cold but the day before she'd seen Christy McCloud at the supermarket with her four-year-old son, Joe. Out of the clear blue Joe asked if Trudy would sit with him in church. She went to bed early the night before so she would be healthy enough to go. She sat with the McCloud family on the second row and listened as Pastor Green went through the service. The crowd was small that morning. First Baptist was losing members, which was part of the reason Johnny was trying a new musical program. More upbeat songs and contemporary music. Acoustic praise songs replaced boring old organ tunes. Some said Johnny had been talking to Iggy about playing drums. Trudy thought the whole thing was ridiculous. She felt God must be praised with the chords and melodies of the old days or it just wouldn't take. Nonetheless she was proud of Johnny for the work he did and she thought Iggy's presence in church each week was a sign that young people weren't as bad as everyone made them out to be.

The events of that morning have been told and retold in the media, in trial transcripts, and through our own investigations. The detail that's always most striking is how quickly it happened. The whole service went as it did each week. A song from the choir and the reading of scripture, the prayers of the people, the offering, another song, the sermon and the benediction.

Iggy was in the back row and walked calmly to the middle of the sanctuary as everyone stood and closed their eyes in prayer. No one noticed he was carrying gasoline.

Slowed down, the terror of that day is difficult to understand. We imagine the congregation deep in prayer. Perhaps praying to an invisible maker to render their future better than their past. More money, less illness, more time. We know what Trudy prayed for that day. She told the court.

I prayed for little Joe McCloud who was sitting next to me, she testified. I prayed he would grow up and walk with Christ.

Iggy was shaking, trying to pour the gasoline, getting it

everywhere. He put the gas can down. A small stream ran down the floorboards to the altar. Then he brought out the matches. He fumbled with the matchbook. Dropping it to the floor. He picked it up and tried again. One lit on fire. He touched it to his shirt, but it went out. Johnny was sitting with the choir. He realized what was happening and ran toward Iggy. Everyone was screaming. Iggy tried another match and this time it lit. But when he saw Johnny running, he panicked and dropped the lit match to the floor. It didn't take long for the two-hundred-year-old pine floors to ignite.

Thick black smoke was everywhere in less than a minute, Trudy testified. Couldn't see your hand in front of your face.

She began to weep on the stand.

I hear those screams at night when I try to sleep, she said. I keep replaying that morning in my mind trying to figure out how to save Johnny and the others. I hate myself for not trying harder.

The lawyer handed her a tissue.

I remembered from fire safety class to stay low, she said. I crawled under the pews until I reached a window and I broke it with a hymnal. I could feel the fresh air on my face and went toward it. I jumped, fell maybe two or three feet. Then I was outside on the grass, on my back. That's when I realized I was holding little Joe McCloud. I don't even remember grabbing him.

They ran across the street and watched the flames get higher. She noticed someone watching the fire. It was Iggy. He was standing there as if nothing had happened, as if he was in a dream.

When the fire trucks arrived, the roof of the church collapsed. The EMTs came but there was no one left to save. All twenty-five worshipers were killed. The police came next. Without being asked, Iggy told them what he had done. Almost in disbelief, they arrested him.

As you sit here today, the lawyer asked Trudy. What do you see when you look at Iggy?

I see a boy that had a lot of potential, she said. That same lost boy I met the first day Johnny brought him home. I've known many young people in my life as an educator. I knew Iggy's type. He had no community. Some young people will seek sex or drugs to soothe them. Iggy sought violence because he couldn't understand a world that he was not the center of. I begged him before, and I'll use my time here to say it to him again: Repent. Give your life to Jesus. Help others do the same. Don't let your life be wasted.

Trudy didn't know where to go after the fire. They took her to the police station. When Joe McCloud's grandparents arrived many hours later, Joe was too afraid to let go of Trudy. When they finally took him from her arms, she broke down. The weight of what happened hit her all at once. The detective in the room kept her from falling. He had been one of her students.

Hold on to me, he said. I won't let you fall.

They took her to the hospital and sedated her. The whole time she kept asking about Joe. The next day every ten minutes a new student from the old days would come by and see her. Former colleagues and friends brought food. So many that the doctors had to restrict the number of visitors. Everyone said she saved Joe's life. The paper called her "the heroic grandma."

After the fire some of Trudy's kin, a cousin and cousin-in-law, had arrived from Alabama, and were caring for her. They'd been reading online about Iggy. They told Trudy that he was at the county courthouse that afternoon for a bond hearing.

I want to go, she said. I want to see him.

I'm not sure that's a good idea, the cousin said. You need your rest.

Trudy drove herself downtown, the cousin insisting on coming along. After much waiting, they brought Iggy into the tiny courtroom in shackles. The judge read some remarks and the lawyers answered some questions. Then the judge asked if anyone from the public wanted to make a statement. Trudy walked to the front of the room. She was wearing a flower-print dress. Her usual teacher demeanor had dropped. People parted as she walked up. Iggy sat with his head forward, looking at the wall. Trudy reached a tiny microphone near where the judge sat.

She looked at Iggy.

I want to say that I loved you, she said. I fought in my heart for you and prayed each day that the Lord would find a path for you. But it seems that Christ didn't win.

She took a deep breath.

You killed the best people, she said. My whole world was in that sanctuary and you took them from me. And for what? What possible reason?

IGGY

2006

1

’M NOT LONG for the world. I still dream about the future even though I don't have one. In six days, I'll be weightless. Murdered by the state. Like a dog chases rabbits in his sleep, I pine for Cleo and Paul. I dream of getting high and shooting roman candles with them from the top of a speeding freight train, racing through the night. I dream of starting revolutions in the streets, dying happy and lonesome in a tiny village faraway. I dream of gladiolus tall as swords in shop windows. Mostly though I dream of walking in the sun. In the bright clear air. On a quiet street. I turn the corner. Someone is calling my name.

Pain becomes meaningless with time. All that's left for me to do is die and I hope they smile when they inject me.

I see my life in reverse. I remember afternoons in North Carolina that felt almost prehistoric. Wandering the woods imagining I could one day build a secret little city for myself. Riding my bike down to the abandoned hospital and breaking stained-glass windows with half bricks. Or the first time I got wine-cooler wasted when I was twelve and held a yellow python at the sketchy pet store. I remember seventh grade. My teacher said she once met Ronald Reagan and no one cared. They moved our class into a trailer where everything smelled like ranch dressing. I remember the sound of the toy guns in the moonlight and listening to my first best friend masturbate in the darkness when he thought I was asleep. I can't even recall his name. His dad was a surgeon. They had a pool table and a wet bar and a movie screen that came down from the ceiling with a remote control. I remember Cleo's orange hair. Her smooth legs the first night we fucked in my Jeep behind the water tower. She fell asleep on my chest. And Paul's dark eyes and thick drawl. We would skip school and drive out to the wild endless countryside and have long conversations about the apocalypse and how maybe every person on earth was actually God.

The one thing that's kept me going all these years is watching the leaves fall. I can see one tree from the tiny window in my cell. I think it's a maple, but could be a cherry or a mulberry or possibly a poplar. Regardless, I think of it as a dogwood. I tell time by the light passing across the room. At night I study the stars in my little sliver of sky and create my own constellations. There's The Sleeping Mockingbird beside The Prize Fighter, which is just beyond The Maestro and The Hitchhiker. My favorite is The Backstroke Swimmer that I can see only in summer. I've been here for almost six years. Isolation becomes so deep that your mind betrays you. Voices crowd you. There's no way to know one season from another except the raging cold or terrible heat. And the tree. It's on a little hill beyond the barbed wire and the highway and the subdivisions.

I remember the day they brought me here. The guards joked about the female agent that dropped me off.

She's a little hottie, one said to the other.

Looked like Winona Ryder, I said. Or that girl from *The Addams Family*.

Christina Ricci, the captain said. Hell yeah she did.

The captain's name is Tom. He's the boss guard. The CO. He's always been good to me cause I'm a skinny dumb kid. Tom hates the tough guys and the Nazis. He knows I'm not in a gang and don't fuck around like that. The Cleveland Bombers are here and the Saudi who tried to light his underwear on fire. Couple of dead-to-rights serial killers, too. Cops treat me kindly, mostly cause I keep to myself. When I got arrested, one officer brought me a Whopper combo from Burger King and a chocolate shake to eat while they did the interview. They asked me about the fire. Guess they're interested in the nature of things. The FBI agent was a sizable man. Wore a comical mustache. Reminded me of my little-league coach who got caught peeping in the showers after practice.

Suppose you think I'm a psychopath or something. You want to know about my family, my early years. Must be something with my upbringing that caused me to go astray. Abusive father, negligent mother. Or perhaps I'm a spurned lover seeking revenge. Or maybe you'll say it was society's fault. Or all that codeine I used to drink and violent movies. Or my political beliefs. But it's none of those things. Or all of those things. You want to know why I did what I did? Might as well take a handful of water and ask if it's river or rain.

I loved two people at the same time. I was rich and poor and sane and insane. I hated and feared people and places and things. My mother was a high-handed drunk and my father was full of gruesome moods. My life was a hurricane and a clear bright bitch of a day. I am the hero and the villain. I am the man who tried to save you.

In a past life I was a guerrilla fighter named Nebuchadnezzar. Fought against my countrymen but not necessarily for the Union. I was on the side of the dispossessed. I charged through generals with my stolen horse and broke their sabers over my knee.

I watch the lone dogwood from my window. Swaying sideways in the wind. Short shadows fill my cell and soon it will be time to sleep. The first day of my last week is coming to an end. I am prepared. I knew it would come to this. I mourn the future I will never know. I dream of one day glimpsing the world from on top. I dream of shouting my name into the valley.

2

WHEN I WOKE UP THIS MORNING, the right side of my body was numb. Thought it might be permanent, but I soon came back to life. Headaches keep me in bed most days and there's been a persistent ringing in my ears for the last six months. The doctor came and checked me over last week. I'm not sure why. Guess to see if I was healthy enough to die.

They put an extra apple with my breakfast. A big green one. Granny Smith, I think. They must be starting to feel sorry for me cause Captain Tom even brought me fresh coffee, too.

How ya feeling, Tom asked.

Good, sir, I said. Better now.

The coffee was warm in my hands and reminded me of drinking decaf early mornings at Sunday school with powdered donuts. Captain Tom was looking at the floor, not like usual. It's strange how people act around a condemned man so close to the end. Like they have some kind of reverence for death.

We're gonna have to talk at some point about some things, he said.

OK, I said.

Your meal, he said. I'll need to know soon so we'll have enough time.

I nodded.

If you haven't thought of any final things to say maybe start now, he said. You don't want to have to think of something last minute.

I've been writing, I said. I should have something ready when the time comes.

All right then, he said.

He acted as though he was going to say something else but he didn't. Then he walked out. The room was quiet again. I looked out the window and could see the dogwood's blossom was almost done falling. The warm summer days were nearly gone and each morning was colder than the last. I wanted to see that last blossom fall. Felt a strange relationship to it. Like it was the final good thing on earth.

I dreamed about Cleo last night and Harmony. The stores downtown and the old blue water tower and the worthless high school. It was a terribly normal place to grow up. I used to go every afternoon to the public library and pick a random book off the shelf and start reading it. That's how I found William Faulkner and Gertrude Stein and Emily Dickinson. I read everything. Books about old sleeper trains from Venice to London and crazy ants in Texas that eat people's TVs. I read about Che Guevara and St. Francis of Assisi and the films of Pasolini. I read about windmills and Catahoula dogs and the Opium Wars.

I was thinking about the library this morning as I ate my

apple, finished the last of the coffee. I went over my dream from the night before. It was one I've had many times about Cleo. We're riding Vespas through a city park and we stop to feed giraffes. It's stupid, I know, but it's all I have. A surrealist painting come to life.

We met my sophomore year, 1997. Her biological parents died when she was young (black ice, country road) so she lived down on Mulberry Street with her godparents. Her new dad was sick with a spinal disease, in a wheelchair ever since I knew him, and her new mom worked at the brick factory as an accountant. I used to ride my bike over there and me and Cleo would watch the airplanes pass on their way south. Harmony must be on some flight path for NASCAR driver's private planes flying into Charlotte. Cleo's house had one of those flat roofs. Kind of a modern place with glass walls. Her dad built it when he was still able to move. We'd watch the planes fly over and guess where they were coming from and talk about all the places we wanted to go.

Those years are so wistful and bizarre. The wind made the azaleas seem as if they hovered six inches off the ground. The neighbor's dogs Salt and Pepper barked like quarreling lovers. Blink my eyes and I'm back in Harmony and the night is clear and the cicadas are electric. I can float above the mountains and fly the path of a dark river to the sea. Cleo is a kind, serious angel that watches over me. I've spent whole months wondering what she's doing out there. Who she's with, where she goes. I can see so clearly the tiny blond hairs that cover the small of her back. Hear her whistle like a butcherbird.

She was a year younger than I was but seemed ancient.

Built small, sad eyes. She reminded me of the circus girl from *La Strada*. Her hair was green the day we first met. In the lunchroom, she was sitting alone. Wearing a pink leather choker and a shirt with a picture of a bloody girl. I walked up to her with idiot confidence.

Who's that girl on your shirt, I asked.

She looked me over. I guess deciding something in her mind. Lord knows what she thought of me. I was kind of going through a psychedelic cowboy phase.

Sit down if you want, she said.

I sat across from her.

Are you a freshman, I asked.

She didn't look up from her food.

It's Carrie, she said.

Who, I asked.

Girl on my shirt, she said. From the movie *Carrie*.

Oh, I said. Never seen it.

She rolled her eyes.

Well, you should, she said and went back to eating.

For the rest of the lunch I didn't know what else to say and so we sat there in silence. It wasn't awkward, actually kind of refreshing. We'd found each other and that was the important thing. A few days later I saw her out behind the gym smoking a cigarette and I asked her for one.

You're doing it wrong, she said. Like this.

She exhaled out of her mouth and inhaled through her nostrils.

French inhale, I asked.

French inhale, she said.

She smiled.

I'm not a total asshole, I said. I just dress like one.

She laughed at that. There's not many things in this world better than a deep pure laugh like hers. Like hearing someone singing gospel or screaming for help. Every day after that I tried to get a laugh out of her. No one else was like her at our school. Sure there were goths and punks, hipsters and goons, but Cleo was different. She never got picked on for the way she dressed. She had a way of dispensing with people she found expendable. I saw huge football players walk on the opposite side of the hallway to avoid her.

One day she invited me to listen to a Lou Reed record at her house. Her bedroom was full of candles. A Courtney Love poster on the wall and a fish tank with no water in it. Wax pooled on the floor in a figure eight.

She told me she was feeling a strange, yet familiar, feeling.

It's something between a continuous longing and a sudden dread, she said. Like a rainy afternoon when the sun is shining or the mysterious hum of an empty street at night.

The Constant, she called it.

Sounds terrifying, I said.

Are you scared, she asked.

She touched my knee.

My mom's at work, she said. Dad's at physical therapy.

I nodded.

Why are you touching my knee, I asked.

She didn't answer.

Then she told me a long, rambling story about how one time

she'd run away from home and met a stranger at a Chinese buffet who wanted to pay her fifty bucks to touch her feet.

What did you do, I asked.

I took off my shoes, she said. While he kissed my feet I stole his wallet. He only had twenty-five dollars in there anyway.

Really, I asked.

Cleo changed the record from Lou Reed to Bach. Some of his sad cello stuff.

You know I'm not exclusive, she said. And I don't like games.

OK, I said.

She was taking off her clothes, quite slowly, almost imperceptibly.

You have a crush on me, she said. Everyone knows it.

Maybe, I said.

That's not what I heard, she said. I heard it was a big, bad serious crush.

When I took her panties off I could see tiny marks where she had cut her inner thighs. I knew better than to ask. I figured it had something to do with The Constant.

We spent the next two years skipping school to seek weird adventures. Mostly we drove around in my old beat-up VW and got high on bad weed. It never felt like a high school romance. It was savage, cosmic, and strange. I was beginning my long slide into a dark place that only got darker. Cleo was mostly what kept me away from the edges. Sex was a weapon we used against The Constant. A barricade against everlasting fear.

I felt The Constant, too. I knew things would never get better. Adults always told us we were too young to understand.

They said we should be happy. I never understood happiness. The whole concept seemed obscene. Nobody in Harmony was even close. All they did was work and go to church. I used to stay up late at night praying for nuclear war. Then I realized no one would ever drop a bomb on Harmony.

Nothing ever happened. Nothing ever changed.

What I thought was trouble back then was simply life. It was neither good nor bad. It just was. I'd give anything for one more night with Cleo. One more memory of her. I've exhausted all the ones I have now. Like the time we saw an Amish man stealing a microwave. Or the time we stayed up all night drinking wine coolers and came face-to-face with a zebra. I always felt that with Cleo somehow the things that were supposed to be dreams were actually real and real life was some kind of nightmare.

Captain Tom brought lunch today, but I didn't eat. Stayed in bed most of the afternoon. He came back in during supper and asked if I wanted to see a priest on Sunday and that my lawyer wanted to talk to me and that they had about fifty media requests. I told him I didn't want to see anyone.

He nodded his head and looked at his shoes. I always liked old Tom and I'll miss him, I really will, I just wish he wouldn't be such a sad sack of shit around me. It was hard to respect a man so down in the mouth.

Any thoughts about what we talked about this morning, he asked.

I reckon a pulled-pork sandwich might be nice, I said. And a Dr Pepper in a bottle.

You got it, he said.

Things changed with me and Cleo the summer after junior year. When I got a job on a landscaping crew. That's when I met Paul. It was the beginning of one thing. The end of something else.

As I fell asleep I started to dream about the last dogwood blossoms falling outside my window and I became them. They became multitudinous and filled the rivers and they filled the oceans and covered every inch of the world.

3

BY THE TIME YOU READ THIS I'll be free of the earth. What does it matter if I've told you the truth? I'll admit that perhaps I've been less than honest. Anyway you wouldn't believe me if I told you the truth. The truth is funny like that. Nothing's ever as real as The Constant circling in the depths. For me, darkness begets darkness and love only got me into trouble.

The summer after junior year was the low point. Every night I snorted painkillers and listened to the music of the night. Freight trains leaving the brick factory. Police cars headed down to Yellow Hill. I bought Vicodin and Xanax from a guy named Memphis down on Park Drive. I crushed them into a fine white powder and rolled it into a cigarette and puffed it out the window. The good life I'd been promised seemed to diminish each evening with the setting sun. The possibilities became smaller and smaller. Tragedy went from a probability, to a likelihood, to an inevitably.

I applied to work with the landscaping crew the day after

school let out for the summer. I wanted Cleo to try to get a job there too, but she said she wanted to stay with her dad. He wasn't doing so well. She was taking a film class at the community college all summer. We watched movies at my place. A few Alfred Hitchcock films and *Taxi Driver* and *Raging Bull*, stuff like that. But also *8½* and *Stalker* and *The Seventh Seal* and a bunch by this Japanese guy named Ozu. I liked his late movies best. They felt like being inside an old man's dream. Whole days early that summer were spent mowing grass and sitting alone in a Hardee's parking lot dreaming of Japan.

The day when Paul first came to work on the crew, it was raining and we all sat in Hardee's. The rest of the guys said he was bad luck for bringing the weather, but I told him not to worry about what they said. He was eighteen, a year older than me. Tan and tall. Tired eyes. He'd just moved to town, his father was the new minister at First Baptist.

We ended up talking about Russia. Not sure why, it was something I'd been reading about the day before at the library and brought it up to him apropos of nothing. He asked if I'd ever heard of the Bolshoi. I mentioned Degas's paintings and he perked up at that. Who were we but two country boys talking about ballet in a fast-food restaurant on a rainy day?

I want to be a choreographer, he whispered.

He said it like it was some kind of dirty idea.

So what, I said.

My father, he said.

Let me guess, I said. He wants you to be an NFL quarterback who flies jets on the weekends.

Something like that, he said.

Paul looked at me for a long time. He was different, like Cleo, but more cosmopolitan. He wore a red bandanna around his neck like a Frenchman and he drank brandy from a sliver canteen. Always reading these thick European history books I'd never heard of and biographies of famous dancers. I saw him walking to work in the morning with his big straw hat and tote bag.

We were always working side by side and spending our lunch breaks together. Those long desperate afternoons at rich people's houses trimming hedges. Planting rose bushes. Paul made the days go by. I used to look inside at those houses and picture myself there, feet up on the coffee table, cold beer in my hand.

Bob was the bossman, a dude not much older than I was. His dad owned the company. He sat in the truck listening to sports radio. Sometimes he'd lean on the hood dipping Skoal with his wraparound sunglasses, whistling at ladies. The rest of the crew was mostly Central and South American guys. There was Eddy and Angel and Luis. They were all much older than I was and liked to play pranks. Angel was the oldest. Probably in his fifties. He was always putting hot sauce in Eddy's water or locking Luis in the Hardee's bathroom with a plastic knife. Bob hated them and called them all kinds of racist names when he was around me and Paul. Like we were supposed to agree with him cause we were white. I never said anything but Paul always told him off. I was too scared to lose my job. Paul didn't give a shit.

The summer went on pretty uneventful. The days of lawnmowers and flowers turned into nights of sad foreign films with

Cleo. Then one weekend I called her and she couldn't come over so I called Paul instead. He said his parents were out of town on a church retreat and their lake house was empty.

It was one of those blue fantastic afternoons. Paul drove over in his father's yellow Mustang. We went ninety miles an hour down to the lake through the countryside listening to Howlin' Wolf. Paul was wearing an unbuttoned Hawaiian shirt and his straw hat. I wore overalls with no shirt and a pair of aviator sunglasses. We stopped on the side of the road to watch a horse nuzzle his newborn. Sipped brandy under a hundred-year-old oak tree and snorted painkillers in a Wendy's drive-through. Shared a Frosty as we waited for a long train to pass. We were so high we bought five watermelons at a farmers market. It was almost dark by the time we got to his lake house. A huge place with tons of rooms and an outdoor shower. We drank some expensive wine and smoked a joint out on the porch.

Then Paul showed me down into the basement where his dad kept his guns. There was a safe with all sorts of weapons and porn. He handed me an assault rifle and some ammo. We set up the watermelons on the dock and shot them through the scope. It felt good to have the gun in my hand. The pure power scared me and I loved it. We spent the rest of the daylight drinking and laughing and shooting random things in the trees. Paul made steaks on the grill and we ate them overlooking the water. I was pretty fucked up and I could tell Paul was getting there too. Then he asked if I wanted to take the boat out.

We changed clothes and went out on the water. He took me

to a secluded beach and we jumped in. We spread out towels on the sandbar and warmed ourselves under the young moon.

You have a girlfriend, he said.

You mean Cleo, I asked.

He nodded and moved over closer to me.

Can I ask you something, he said.

What, I asked.

He looked out over the water.

Never mind, he said and laid back.

We sat there for a long time not saying anything. Wind filled the trees and stopped. My heart was pounding. Paul's eyes were closed. I inched closer to him, not sure what I wanted to happen. He stood up and started to walk toward the boat. I grabbed his hand and pulled him close to me.

Ask me what you were going to ask me, I said.

He kissed me instead. It was slow and easy with Paul. He was patient with me. We spent the night at the lake house making love. The next morning we rode back to town and went to work on Monday. I couldn't look at him the same.

When I get to this part of the story, people always ask me if Cleo was jealous of Paul or if Paul was jealous of Cleo. I never understood that, though. All three of us had something in common. We'd been told that we weren't like the rest of the world. That something inside us was missing. We became each other's medicine against the weariness.

We all three made plans to meet at Paul's lake house one Saturday afternoon. The week was long and hot and I couldn't wait for it to end. On Friday, we were working in Mayor Presley's yard. Angel was up on the hillside Weed-Eating. Bob was sitting in the truck talking on the phone. I was trimming a hedge when I looked up at Angel and he was on his back. I turned to Paul.

Look at Angel, I said. He fell.

The other guys started laughing. Thought it was one of his pranks. I laughed too and went back to work. Then I looked back up again and saw Angel hadn't moved.

I don't think he's joking, I said to Paul.

Paul went up the hill and stood over him. He yelled down for help. Everyone dropped their tools and ran toward him. Bob poked his head out of the truck.

Hey, he said. What are you doing?

Angel fell, I said.

I don't care, he said. Get back to work.

Paul ran into Mayor Presley's house and called an ambulance. I ran to Angel, started giving him CPR. I didn't really know how to do it. The whole time Bob was telling everyone to get back to work. When the EMTs got there, Angel was already gone. They loaded him up and drove away. There was no big fanfare. Nobody wailing and moaning. He just died alone on a hill.

It was the first time I really saw a dead person up close like that. One minute you were here and the next you weren't. I tried to find out where the funeral was going to be but Luis said they were going to ship his ashes back to Honduras and that was that.

The next day I picked Paul and Cleo up to go to Paul's lake

house. On the drive down Cleo and Paul didn't say a word to each other.

We pulled up to the house.

Pretty nice, Cleo said. Your dad in the mob or something?

He's a minister, I said.

Same thing, Cleo said.

We went out on the boat. Cleo rolled us cigarettes all afternoon. Paul made bourbon and ginger ales. Then we went back into that little cove and watched a rainbow arrive over the sandbar. Cleo took pictures with her Polaroid camera. A late summer dream.

As we pulled up to the dock, Paul's parents were there waiting. His dad was wearing a FISHERMAN FOR JESUS hat and a big metal watch, his mom was in yoga pants. They were pissed cause Paul told them he was at my house spending the night. They'd planned a romantic getaway and thought someone had broken in and stolen their boat.

Someone got into the gun safe, Paul's dad said. Was that you, too?

He decided to search us for drugs, which he found. Then he searched Cleo's bag and found pictures of me and Paul kissing. I think about that day often. How if maybe we'd taken another lap around the lake something would've been different. Or if we'd never gone to the lake that day in the first place.

My cell is ice-cold as I write this. I'm getting tired thinking about the past. I wish I had more to say. Something profound to leave you with but there's only the cold creeping in. Captain Tom brought me my dinner.

On Saturday we move you to a small holding cell, he said. It's procedure.

Do you think I'll still be able to see the dogwood tree from my window, I asked.

He looked at me for a second and shook his head.

No window, he said.

— 4 —

SUPPOSE YOU WANT to know about Johnny Nightshade. The first time I met him he beat me up with his saxophone. I was in the parking lot of the library, weeping. It was hot. Almost the Fourth of July. Johnny Nightshade wasn't his real name, of course, but that's what everyone called him. He was a local musician that played street-corner jazz every night downtown. In his fifties, he was the town's only busker. Leftover from a bohemian world that never really reached Harmony. A resident alien from a different time and place, soul patch and cabbie hat in a town full of football jerseys and mullets. He was beloved in a way because of a curious loophole in evangelicalism whereby you had to be friends with anyone who played music at church regardless if they looked stupid or not. And Johnny could undeniably play the shit out of that saxophone. The very saxophone he beat me up with.

But I'm getting ahead of myself. After the incident at the lake, Paul's father sent him away to rehab camp and there things only got worse. He fell in with people that exposed him to harder stuff than we were doing. I was unemployed at the time. Bob fired everybody after Angel's death. I dropped out of school and was spending most of my days in the computer room drinking gin and orange juice cause it was all that I could keep down. I was watching videos until all hours. Random stuff at first, but soon it became darker. Plane crashes, police shootings, suicides, beheadings. The Constant made manifest. Maybe I was so numb I wanted to feel something, even if it was other people's pain.

Paul used to send me these rambling letters from rehab about how he would go on long swims in the lake and think about moving to Europe. He thought America was too far gone and that we were basically living at the end of civilization. He was reading more about revolutionary anarchists. Cleo was still in school. We met at the Starlight Diner one morning for blueberry pancakes. She talked about wanting to make a documentary about the invisible things that control our world. She'd dyed her hair blonde and pierced her nose. We sat in a booth by the window.

Do you ever feel like doing something, I asked her.

Like what, she said.

I don't know, I said. Burning everything to the ground.

She rolled her eyes.

You're such a rebel, she said.

I'm serious, I said.

OK, she said. But are you going to finish your pancakes first?

I slid her my plate.

Some weekends we'd drive up in the mountains and trail-ride horses when we could scrape together the cash. We'd camp by the Bluebird River and make love beside a longleaf pine. But the days had become too much for me. The tedium unbearable. I found myself joyless at breakfast still drunk after a night in front of the computer. Then, I guess it was after a fight with my mom, I started to look up ways to kill myself. I found this forum where people were talking about it. At first it was almost a joke. See what these idiots were on about, but then I began to understand them. They all wanted to die but they didn't want to die in vain. There didn't seem to be any glory left in the world. A sickness had infected everything.

I got a letter from Paul one day. He was coming back to Harmony. Wanted to party. I suggested we meet at the old water tower at midnight. Cleo picked me up after her class and we drove out there under big stars. The moon hung above us, just a thumbnail. We smoked cigarettes and listened to a Dostoevsky audiobook. Made bets about if Paul would really show. Finally he did arrive in a van with a few other people from his rehab. It didn't take long to realize they had escaped. We spent three days under the rusted old water tower listening to Neil Young, eating homemade tacos, and shooting heroin. It was my first time and wasn't what I expected. Like God ran his finger down my spine, that's what it was. All my pain transmogrified into a star. I could've lived like that for years but after three days our luck ran out. Paul's father found him and called the cops. They arrested him and when they put him into the car, somehow I knew. I knew it was the last time I'd see him. I remember him standing there handcuffed. Just standing there, waiting. There's always waiting with cops. They can't do anything in a timely manner. Paul shot me a glance.

He laughed and tried to wave.

Love you, I said.

I'll call you when I'm out, he said.

And that was it. The last words he spoke to me. Two days later he was out of jail and I called his house and his father called me a faggot and told me never to call there again. Paul told everyone he was going into the merchant marines. Instead, the next day he parked behind RadioShack and overdosed.

I was sitting in the library and got a call from Cleo.

Are you alone, she said.

Yes, I said.

It's Paul, she said.

What happened, I asked. Where is he?

I knew by her silence he was dead. There was nothing else to say.

I believe there's a weird magnetism that exists in the universe. It brings people together and it takes them from this earth. Paul came and left the way a storm comes over the countryside and leaves in the blink of an eye. I walked out into the library parking lot, into the sun. The heat was baking the pavement and the trees were blurry. I wanted to die. I sat in my car with AC on full blast and wept for hours like a child.

Soon I heard the sound of jazz. I rolled down the window.

Knock it off, I said to Johnny Nightshade.

He only played louder. I asked again. He kept playing. After everything I said he answered with the sax. Like he was mocking me with his tune. I couldn't take it. I lost it. In a full blind rage I jumped out of the car and ran toward him. In my head this music was the thing that killed Paul and all I had to do was make it stop. The next thing I remember, I was flat on my back and a brass saxophone bell was coming down on my face. He broke two of my teeth out and gave me a concussion.

I woke up in the hospital. Cleo was there with ice cream. I could hear a love song on the radio. It was a golden oldie and reminded me of summer. Suddenly, maybe the drugs I was on, maybe the grief, I had a vision of being on a band trip in eighth grade to Raleigh and seeing the most beautiful woman I'd ever seen sitting in a cafe. I watched her from my hotel window. When she stood to leave I noticed she was pregnant. I was thinking of her when Johnny Nightshade walked into my hospital room. His saxophone safely in its case.

What are you doing here, Cleo asked.

I've come to apologize, he said. I heard about your friend Paul.

My mind was foggy and I didn't know what was real and what wasn't. Also, it seems strange to say it, but that was the first time I remember anyone telling me they were sorry. He seemed genuine. His cabbie hat in his hands.

It's OK, I said.

I'm gonna do whatever it takes, he said. I'm gonna make this up to you.

You can start by leaving him alone, Cleo said.

He looked at her strangely. The way a mailman looks at a ferocious dog. Then he turned to me. I was tired of being angry.

Sick with pain. Exhausted. I missed Paul more than anything.

I forgive you, I said.

From that day on, I became friends with Johnny. We played chess together downtown. Talked about life. He'd tell me about his time as a professional hitchhiker in the seventies and I'd tell him about the facts I learned from the library. About how some birds can sleep as they fly and how the 1881 earthquake in Lake Springs, Arkansas, made the Mississippi River run backward and the bells in Boston ring. He introduced me to his mother, Trudy. She was in her seventies and they lived together in an old crumbling farmhouse near the edge of town. His father had died a few years before.

Johnny could see how I was hurting. He understood the pain of losing someone. It was as if Paul's death changed something in the order of the universe. It made room for Johnny to come into my life. He told me he channeled the despair of losing his father into music. We were playing chess one afternoon downtown. It was almost winter and he was wearing a long coat and a scarf.

Sometimes I can't shake the emptiness, I said.

He nodded, seemed to know exactly what I was telling him.

I used to fly big planes when I was in the Air Force, he said. You didn't have time to be scared you were too busy flying.

What do you mean, I asked.

That's why I took up the sax, he said. I'm too concerned about finding the next note to worry about my life.

I don't have anything like that, I said.

That afternoon he took me down to Hubert's pawnshop and bought me a used set of drums. I told him I couldn't accept them but he insisted. We set them up in his old barn and played through the winter beside a kerosene heater. We played Charlie Parker and riffed off Coltrane and Brubeck.

That weekend, after a jam session in his barn, Johnny said he'd booked us a gig at a coffee shop in High Point. We drove through a blizzard to get there and five people showed up. By the time we got home, he said I should just sleep over at his place. He made me a room upstairs and his mom made us tea. For once, I felt comfortable. Like I wasn't so untethered from the earth.

I drifted off to sleep but was woken up in the middle of the night. I opened my eyes. Johnny was in his underwear at the door.

Everything OK, he asked.

Fine, I said.

I didn't think much of it so I went back to sleep. Then deep in the night I woke up and Johnny was in my bed. His hand was down my pants.

What are you doing, I yelled.

I jumped out of bed.

I thought you might be cold, he said. Sometimes it's good to sleep together on winter nights.

Get out, I said.

I'm sorry, he said. I thought you—

Go, I said.

The next day I didn't say a word. We acted as though nothing had happened. I didn't say anything to anyone. He just took me home. It was too embarrassing. Johnny kept calling and calling but I wasn't picking up. I started to spend my nights in the computer room again watching death videos and drinking myself to sleep.

One morning I woke up to find my parents in my room.

We need you to come downstairs, my father said.

Johnny and another woman were sitting in the living room.

What's this, I asked.

I'm Debra, the woman said. I'm from a group called Christian Recovery that seeks to intervene with troubled youths.

We love you, Johnny said. We want what's best for you.

What are you talking about, I asked.

The drinking, Debra said. The homosexuality. The drugs. The searches on the family computer.

I'm feeling ambushed, I said. I need to go.

Johnny put his hand on my knee.

We've got this, he said. You can trust us.

— 5 —

MY NAME IS NEBUCHADNEZZAR and I ride through life bareback on wild ponies. The wind speaks my name on mornings when the mist makes the countryside seem heavenly and rare. The river is my last best friend and war is my enemy. I wait until midnight to crush philistines in their sleep. Raid the villages and burn patriarchs in their beds. My horse is immortal, calico and fast, born on the Fourth of July.

My father was killed by a beesting, my mother died from grief. And so I made my way through the mad world as a scavenger of knowledge. Taught myself to read. Learned the mathematics of the stars. Lied to enter college at age sixteen and graduated with honors. I moved to Harmony and lived amongst the highborn all day and the lowlifes all night. Untethered from polite society, I partied with everyone. Gentlemen and ladies, farmhands and milkmaids. Then one morning I saw the great Cardinal train out of Greensboro and I hitched a ride west. In the territory, I lived with sad gauchos and learned the ways of the horse. There was a border war going and I serviced the lusty soldiers home on leave and their lonely wives back at the homesteads. When the conflict was over, I got on as a brakeman headed back east and worked my way up. Moved back to Carolina with a nice little nest egg and an occupation I revered.

I became a conductor on the night trains to Asheville, all speed and steel. I waved my hat in the wind like a fool every night under weird constellations. Came home tired with coal on my face. I believed the righteous word of Jesus at that point. Mother Mary was my mother. The Holy Ghost was my friend. That was until the war came and stole everything from me. A smoldering hellscape from here to the sea and the rich still rich and the poor still dying. The rebels were weak millionaires who forced the country boys to kill on their behalf. I was dragged into the conflict after the rebels took over my farm to use as a barracks and the Unionists burned it to the ground. Now I fight both sides. At night I play the banjo around a big fire.

Champagne is scarce but I drink it when I can. For example, say I kill a man and take over his mansion and throw a big party. I'll bust out the big magnums from the cellar and toast to the end of the world. I dream of a utopia for all mankind where love is legal and the champagne falls like rain.

Let me tell you how I lost my faith. It was winter when I saw both sides of the war let their soldiers freeze to death. Each night through my scope I saw the night watchmen become like statues and they'd bury the poor sucker in the morning and put another boy at his post. Meanwhile, the generals and colonels slept warm in their tents with fires kept going through the night by another poor boy. I thought no man who loves Jesus would let this kind of misery continue. Now you might be saying, but Neb surely you saw worse out in the field of battle. Guts spilled and eyeballs rolling out of heads. It's true, I saw those things and many more. But I retained my stupid faith because I thought it was in service of something greater. When I saw how the officers treated their own soldiers I knew it was part of the Big Lie.

I'm now low most days and haven't brushed my teeth. I let my beard become wild and my mind ripple and hum. At dusk I plan an attack and by night I play my tunes. Happy as a bluebird in a bluebird tree.

Then one night I'm out marauding and there's a cotillion in a big house. I watched through my scope on the hill. I watched for ways to burn them alive. Where to light the blaze, how best to lock the bastards inside. I walked down the hill to get a closer look. I was gathering my matches and kerosene when a dancing couple caught my eye. They were lovely in a tender way, desperate and happy in the moonlight, and I could sense they were caught up in another world. They despised the money and the sin. They could've been anywhere in the world at any time and it would be the same. I knew them like I knew myself because I was them. The grief they wore was my grief because they were missing the same thing I was missing. I knew what I had to do. I went back to the cave and changed into my tuxedo and trimmed my unruly whiskers. Under my long coat I secured two repeater pistols and an ammo belt.

Inside there was a string quartet playing songs of the Romantic period and a long table of finger foods. I helped myself and made my way to the dance floor. The room was crowded with rich boys who dared not lift a finger for the war except to finance it. In the corner was the owner of the place. I knew him only as Fizgerald. He came to me and asked my name.

I'm from Harmony, I said. A gentleman like you.

Who are your people, he asked. Do I know them?

I nearly shot him dead right there, but I knew better.

I'm the third McMillan son, I lied.

I went to school with old Pierce McMillan, he said. Thought his third son died at Chattooga.

Thought wrong, I said. I survived.

Welcome to Shady Oaks, he said. I want you to meet my son and his new wife.

He took me to the couple I had seen through the window. Light fell on them in halos. Up close I knew it was them. Although they had different names, I knew I would see them again in another life.

I took their hands and brought them to my face.

This is Pierce McMillan the third, Fizgerald said.

Don't bring up the war, Paul said. I can't stand to think of it.

I wish it was all over and we lost, Cleo said.

I brought their arms around me and we danced a lascivious dance. In the middle of the song I brought them close to my face and kissed them both. The patrons looked at us, disgusted. An old woman retched in a punch bowl. More than one moved to break us apart. The whole room was whispers and gestures. I recognized one man as a former customer. He went to Fizgerald and pointed my way.

I whispered to Cleo and Paul.

Stay close to me when the deal goes down, I said. We won't have much time.

It was then that Fizgerald approached me and grabbed my collar.

You are not in fact the third McMillan son, he said. You're the criminal and anarchist named Nebuchadnezzar.

Nonsense, I said.

I took his champagne from him and hushed the music.

Long live everything, I toasted.

Then I shot a random man between the eyes. Next I fired the gun at Fitzgerald's chest but he dodged and it grazed him. He moved for his rifle. I shouted to Cleo and Paul to run for my horse outside. I locked the doors. I lit the fuse and we rode away into the night.

We spent six months on the run. Fitzgerald survived the blast and sent a posse into the mountains to find and kill me. For many weeks we lived in bliss, Paul and Cleo and me. Making triple love to each other under falling dogwood blossoms. Drinking fresh water from the river. Shooting deer and wild hogs for supper. It was a grand old time and I cherished the days.

Near the end of the last month Paul fell sick with fever and I could not find a doctor in time. We buried him near an apple orchard and nearly died of sadness. It was only me and my pony and Cleo then, alone in the forest.

I want to escape, she said. But I have no home left to go to. No living kin.

I have done this, I said. I will have to kill again.

No, she said. No more death.

She rested her head on my shoulder as we watched a gathering storm.

Why do you keep calling me Cleo, she asked. It's not my name.

It will be some day, I told her.

Then a bullet went through her eye and she slumped dead. Our camp had been discovered. It was a five-hour gunfight and I killed nine of their men but in the end they caught me. I waited for my hanging in a prison with only my sorrows and dreams. They put me in with defectors and I slept there for four days and nights.

Then the storm came. Out of nowhere I heard the old familiar sound of a steam engine but there were no tracks nearby. It was a twister and it was coming straight for the prison camp. The guards ran in fear and left their posts unmanned. The winds blew down the doors and broke the chains and we all ran out into the storm and some were sucked away into the sky. Although I was weak from scamp food and water I managed to find my way to the road and ran until I found a creek and spent the night. I winked at Jesus and saw a shooting star and lived happily ever after.

This is what I dream of on the last night of my life. Captain Tom moved me into the holding cell, where there is no window. I'm on suicide watch. They don't want me doing it before the government gets their shot. Lately I've been thinking about my end and what words I should say. I can't conceive of what the darkness will be like. I only hope Paul and Cleo are there. I hope they have forgiven me.

6

WOULD LIKE TO PUT A FEW things straight. After my
little intervention with Johnny and Debra from Christian
Recovery my parents sent me off to the same rehab camp
Paul went to. It was a church-sanctioned place. Deeply cruel.
They locked us up together for days in cabins. The teachers
fought us. If we tried to leave, they made us sleep outside with
broken jaws and dislocated shoulders. If someone was caught
drinking or smoking they were locked in the dark for twen-
ty-four hours. The mind begins to fracture without stimula-
tion. You begin to hallucinate. That's when I first began to see
my own past lives.

They selected a few of the boys to work in the faculty house.
If you wanted special treatment you had to get in good with Dr.
Rex, the headmaster. He wasn't a real doctor. Had a PhD in
theology from some Baptist college. They'd set this place up in
an old summer camp. When I first arrived we were woken up at
5 a.m. every morning and made to run for miles through the

woods before breakfast. We worked long hours in a call center selling Christian vacation packages to the Holy Land. But after the first month I was moved to the headmaster's house staff. We did the laundry and cleaned his rooms. Then he asked me one day to help him with his back. At first it wasn't anything too bad. I'd rub one spot on his back and he would thank me. But for days and days that's all he'd talk about. How I'd worked wonders on him.

He asked me to come to his room one Sunday night after Bible study. When I walked in, he took his shirt off. He told me to use oil. I knew it was weird but it was better than night exercises. When I was done, he told me to wait downstairs while he showered.

I'm surprised you didn't find this already, he said.

He pulled a Dr. Pepper from the fridge and opened it, poured us both a glass. He let me watch TV for an hour and ordered us a pizza. He turned the TV off and we sat awkwardly in his living room.

I got to go back to the dorm, I said.

Suit yourself, he said.

As I left he thanked me again. Told me he'd never felt better. He patted me on the back.

This was great, he said. But I think we better keep this night between me and you. Wouldn't want the other boys to get jealous.

Sure, I said.

Things went back to normal. Work detail. Exercise. Bible study. But a few weeks later he asked me to come back again. He ordered another pizza. We sat on the couch and watched

Law and Order. An old episode where a maid's body is found under a bed in a sleazy motel. After it was over, I stood up to leave.

Maybe you could tell me a little about yourself, Dr. Rex said.

I should get back, I said. I'll get in trouble.

You're with me, Dr. Rex said. Don't worry.

I sat back down on the couch.

I felt The Constant deeply and I tried to move through it. The weeks became months. The outside world faded and the camp became my existence. I had a persistent fever that I couldn't shake. I wasn't sure what Dr. Rex wanted from me. It felt as though I was moving when I was sitting still.

Dr. Rex went to the kitchen and came back with a gift.

I know it's hard to be away from home on your birthday, he said. Happy eighteenth.

I opened it. It was a pair of drumsticks.

We don't have drums here, he said. But at least you can practice rudiments in your bunk.

The fever washed over me again. I'd never felt such heat. I wanted to call Cleo. I wanted to hear her voice. Harmony came back to me. All the long old nights.

Tell me about Paul, Dr. Rex said. We've never talked about him.

What about him, I asked.

He refilled my glass.

Paul's father is a close friend of mine, he said.

Oh, I said.

Pastor Green told me everything, he said.

I looked out the window and could see moonlight on an empty field. At the edge of it was a scarecrow that looked crucified. I didn't know what to say.

I know you were the one who gave him the drugs, he said.

No, I said. You've got it wrong.

Dr. Rex put his arm around me.

All you have to do is ask for forgiveness, he said.

I looked out the window again but the scarecrow was gone. Or maybe he'd just faded into the shadows. My fever was high and moving higher. I'd never felt The Constant as I did at that moment. I wanted to tell Dr. Rex everything. How it was Paul's father that caused all this. I wanted to tell him how Johnny had tried to touch me. But I knew he wouldn't believe me. I'd remembered a book I'd pulled off the shelf years before about monks that would light themselves on fire in protest. And the lines of an old zen poem about cremation: *I had great joy in my body. Scatter the ashes.*

I made a plan at that moment. I hugged Dr. Rex and began to cry.

I want mercy, I said. I want the grace of Jesus.

He pulled away.

You're burning with fever, he said. I'm taking you to the infirmary.

I went to sleep that night on a cot in the infirmary and dreamed of a million crucified versions of myself. I dreamed white phosphorus blossoming into flame. The earth shook inside me and I found myself in the rubble. The sky became black with smoke and the ash fell like snow. I woke the next morning and the nurse told me I'd been asleep almost a full day.

Some folks from a ministry in Harmony are coming today, she said.

I'm from Harmony, I said.

Oh, she said. Then you must know them.

When Pastor Green and Johnny got to campus I showed them around. I talked about how I had seen the light. I was off drugs and didn't have the same lusts anymore. Pastor Green was impressed. That night I had a Bible study with them and told him I was sorry for what I'd done. He put his hand on my shoulder and smiled.

You remind me of Paul, he said.

By the end of the weekend, I'd convinced Pastor Green and Johnny to let me come back to Harmony. Told them I wanted to work for the church.

For months I worked at First Baptist and did everything they asked me. I went to every service and prayer meeting. At the same time, I put my plan together. I dreamed of the monk on fire. The night before I put my plan in action, Cleo came over. We watched a noir movie on TV. She'd dyed her hair red and gotten a job at the library. We smoked a little and made out. She rolled over on top of me and drummed on my chest a little beat.

I have to tell you something, I said.

What, she said. Your whole Christian thing is an act. I already know that.

No, I said. Well, yes. But there's more. I have a plan.

What, she asked.

I'm going to light myself on fire, I said. Tell the world about The Constant.

Cleo laughed.

Call me tomorrow, she said.

She gave me a long kiss goodbye. That was the last time I saw her.

The next morning I dressed and got the gas can from the garage and put it in a duffle bag and drove to Sunday morning church service. Pastor Green gave a sermon on the price of sin and Johnny Nightshade played his songs. Everyone closed their eyes for the final prayer.

I walked down to the middle of the sanctuary and poured gasoline on myself. I didn't want to die peacefully. I wanted to roar up in flames. It seems stupid now, but I thought if I was on fire they would have to listen to me. But no one ever listened. Some of the gasoline had splashed in my eyes. Blinded me a second. I fumbled for the matches in my pocket. I tried to say something final and profound. Announce my grief. Proclaim meaningfully about The Constant, but I couldn't get anything out. I remember Johnny running toward me and I accidentally dropped the match and the floor caught. I thought the fire would destroy me but all it did was remind me how beautiful things actually were. How simple and good. I didn't want to die anymore. It happened so fast. I fucked it all up. One minute I was in the sanctuary choking on smoke, the next I was outside breathing the cool August air.

I say the names of the dead each night before I sleep. Beg for the mercy that I don't deserve. I pray to a godless universe, my knees on the hard floor.

My life won't really end at midnight because it ended a million times before. I'm not sure why but somehow it ended the day Angel dropped dead. And it ended when Paul's dad found the photo. And it ended when I entered that church. And it ended the day I was born into this world. And it ended ten thousand years ago.

My lawyers tried to bring up mental illness. And they wanted me to testify at sentencing about how I didn't mean to burn the church down. They said it would perhaps give some of the jury a way to feel for me. How it was a bad accident. They might not give me the death penalty. But I didn't want anyone to know about that stuff.

It all had to do with The Constant. Something about time and time's best friend, impermanence. The beauty and tragedy of a falling dogwood blossom, it had something to do with that. I've decided my final words will be along those lines. Something about how life fails us all in the end.

I'm still thinking about the future even now. I miss Cleo. I miss Paul. I hurt them too, don't forget that. I did horrible things. I hit my mother once and I wrecked a stranger's car and I stole three grand from my father to buy drugs. I missed seeing my grandfather's funeral because I didn't want to stop playing video games when I was fourteen. I killed and will be killed.

It wasn't always good, it wasn't always bad.

Things become clearer at the end. Life was what I did between sunrise and sunset. It's weird how we exist like this. It's like when I was a kid I used to love to ride the train to Asheville. I always went to the last car. I watched the track behind me and the way the landscape would come into view. The lonely towns would come into view then disappear in the distance. I used to dream of living in one of those small towns. I guess Harmony would've been just as good.

I don't have any dreams left. All my fear is gone. What's on my mind though isn't the moment of death. It's those train rides from my childhood. They remind me of my first friend and his mom who died. She was a long-distance runner who wore blue bandannas in her hair. She used to have this station wagon and the backseat was turned around and faced out the big back window. That's what I'm thinking about. That feeling of moving forward but only being able to see behind you.

Midnight will be my last midnight. The constellations, I can imagine them each in their place. The dogwood tree, too. I will not see the final blossoms fall. Captain Tom came in and told me my lawyer was here and a priest and I told him to tell them to leave. I have no use for the law or religion anymore. I ate my pulled-pork sandwich earlier this evening. I asked for a cold beer at the last minute and Captain Tom managed to sneak me up a Miller High Life. I sat sipping it thinking of the thousands like it I drank and the thousands more I would never drink. I kept reading the word *life* over and over until it had no more meaning. What a dumb thing it is to die.

I'm not sure who will read this. Maybe they'll destroy it with all my other things or maybe it'll end up in some poor stranger's hands. The ramblings of a murderer. I'm OK with whatever they say about me. I know the truth is always more complicated. It's now two minutes till midnight. Captain Tom is here. It's time to go. I'll just say this in closing. If you've got something you love, hold it close cause there's no telling when they'll come and take it away.

FARBER

~2005~

1

FARBER RODE HIS YELLOW SCOOTER through downtown Harmony sporting a brand-new black fedora he'd ordered online. When he was younger he often wore faint white powder on his face and sometimes, when the mood struck him, black lipstick, too. People in town called him Marilyn Manson, though he preferred Morrissey. A long red scar ran down his chest, breastbone to navel. The result of an emergency surgery when he was only a week old. Back then they believed you could be too young for anesthesia. For years when he closed his eyes at night he dreamed the slow scalpel cutting his skin again. He'd never confessed to anyone that he remembered the pain and no one ever asked.

It was summer again, the heat had returned. Farber took a right on Center Street as the sun crawled just above the horizon. He'd worked at the library for a few months and was about to make full-time because they couldn't find anyone else who knew the computer system. Officially he was hired as the IT guy but after only a short time he thought of himself as running the place. The head librarian, Karen, was a rare idiot. She talked endlessly about conspiracy theories and had a near universal loathing of other people. She had been the only holdover from the old library, which they imploded in a big show that Karen refused to attend because she said it was just a stupid building, blow it up already.

The new library was three stories, modern glass, the top floor was Karen's office and the town archives. The main floor on ground level held the circulation desk, public computers, and the children's books. The children's section had a sweeping mural of a dragon and princess. Someone had donated an old claw-toothed bathtub and it was Farber's idea to fill it full of pillows so the kids could read inside it. Upstairs on the second floor were the rest of the stacks, and spaces where people could read. Sometimes addicts looking for a place to nod off would crash upstairs in the history section. Farber would have to shoo them away before closing. He spent most of his day helping people with the internet. They came in to look up all sorts of things. From bank notices to quicksand porn. He spent his hours behind the circulation desk monitoring their web searches. Karen told him to block any site he deemed inappropriate. Unless one of the autistic kids got into something really hardcore, he usually let it slide. Long ago he'd abandoned any sense of shame or morality. A rabid insomniac, Farber lived his life from an early age almost completely online. He'd found a community of people seeking comfort from reality. When he was online, he was in control. The real world offered too many opportunities for humiliation and regret. Online, if he tired of his personality, he'd simply change his username and become someone else. As a child, in the long lonely hours alone in his room when he couldn't sleep, he looked up the worst things he could think of. These days to combat his insomnia he'd fallen into a strict routine. After his mother fell asleep upstairs, he lived inside a game online most of the night. His avatar was a nymph with fire eyes. He roamed the forests and when his mystic journeys ended, he'd sleep for a few hours. Wake up at 7:00 a.m., eat two breakfast Hot Pockets, and ride his scooter to work.

When Farber pulled into the parking lot of the library, Karen's car was already there. He thought sometimes she slept in it overnight. Always in the same spot. The light in her office was on. It was still a little dark outside. Near the door sat a young woman in a blue bonnet and ankle-length dress with a toddler on her hip. The morning was still cool, but the fog was burning off. Farber recognized her as one of the Yellow Children of God. They were a Christian cult started in the seventies in the county. Their members gave up all their worldly goods to follow an obscure German theologian. The women wore Amish-style long dresses and the men had black hats and beards. They were rarely seen in town without others from their group. He smiled at her and walked to the front door and opened it with his key card.

Finally, the woman said. I've been out here for hours.

We don't open for another ten minutes, Farber said.

I need to use the bathroom, she said.

He looked at the baby, it had some kind of crust around its mouth.

Fine, Farber said. But my boss is upstairs. Stay quiet.

The woman elbowed her way inside. She rushed to the bathroom and locked the door behind her. Farber set his stuff on the table and began to put away the books that the weekend shift didn't finish shelving on the second floor. The phone rang at the front desk. He ran to answer it.

Library, he said. Can I help you?

Have you made the coffee yet, Karen said.

She was calling from upstairs.

Not yet, Farber said.

When you've got coffee, come upstairs, she said. We need to talk.

OK, he said and hung up.

He made a strong pot of coffee in the break room and put it in Karen's oversized mug. As he walked to the elevator and pushed the button the woman and her child came out of the bathroom. The child was crying but the woman didn't seem to notice or care. She had changed out of the long dress and now wore cut-off jean shorts and a blue tank top, still in her bonnet. The child wore only a diaper.

Do these computers work, the mother asked. I need to use the computer.

Farber was struck suddenly by how much skin she was showing.

Yes, he said. Well, yes. They work, the computers, but not yet, actually. I mean, I have to turn them on.

OK, she said. Can you turn them on or not?

Yeah, he said. I mean, we're not technically open yet—

Maybe you can make an exception, she said.

She turned and took off the bonnet and the dull fluorescent bulbs revealed her face. For the first time Farber noticed that she had two different colored eyes. One brown, one blue. Her head was shaved into a close buzz and she had what looked like a homemade figure-eight tattoo on the back of her neck. She was dark tan in the face but nowhere else, as if she worked outside all day. Farber realized she was not much older than he was, maybe two or three years. Never before had he been all alone so close to a woman so beautiful, wearing so little, carrying on like this. Her nipples poked out of her shirt, she wore no bra, and when she bent down to put her child on the floor, he could see her breasts fully. At home Farber fantasized constantly and his fantasies mostly involved fictional characters. Now with this strange real woman in front of him, he no longer had control of anything. He hated the air between them.

Are you going to turn the computers on, she asked.

I need to take this coffee upstairs, he said. For my boss.

Jesus Christ, she said.

Sorry, he said.

He got in the elevator and as the door closed, he took out an inhaler and took a big hit. The doors opened on the third floor and he walked down the hall to Karen's office. She was listening to Rod Stewart on a tiny CD boom box, reading scribbled notebook papers on her desk, peeling an orange.

Sorry for the hold up, he said. I brought your coffee.

She said nothing and kept reading.

He wondered if he should sit down but instead he looked around at the things in her office. Pictures of her fat husband.

Books about self-improvement. Faded numbers from half marathons she'd run decades ago. A poster of a tiger that said PROCRASTINATION KILLS sat unframed on the floor.

Coffee, she said. Give it to me.

He handed it to her.

We need to talk, she said without looking up. I need to cut back your hours.

But I was about to make full-time, he said.

That was the plan, she said. But we've hit a snag with your health insurance.

What kind of snag, he asked.

They said you've got some expensive condition, she said. That puts you in an extremely high-risk pool.

When I was a baby I had this surgery on my heart, he said.

Karen held up her hand.

I don't need to know your medical history, she said. I just need you to work the hours without the benefits.

That doesn't really seem fair, he said.

Karen looked at him now, confused at his ignorance.

I've got to get checkups to monitor my heart condition, Farber said. Expensive scans every six months.

Karen held up her hand.

I don't want to know if you're dying, she said. Are you dying?

Not right now, Farber said.

Can you work the hours or not, she asked.

Sure, he said.

He took the elevator downstairs and hit the inhaler again. The woman was asleep in one of the big reading chairs with her daughter now. Farber unlocked the front door and began to turn on each computer. The first people to arrive were returning books and then people began to sit at the computers and a few mothers with children came in and went to the children's section. The day went by like many others for Farber with the exception of the strange woman. At around noon Karen came down to cover the front desk while he went to get lunch downtown.

Don't dawdle, she said. I've got things to do.

He went to the Starlight Diner and got a cheeseburger and a milkshake and brought it back to eat at the front desk. When he finished his meal he looked over and saw the sleeping woman was gone and he figured she'd left, just another napper looking for somewhere cool to pass the hot hours, but as soon as he had the thought *I'll never see her again* she appeared from the bathroom.

Why didn't you tell me the computers were working, she said.

I didn't want to wake you, he said.

She smiled at him. He was frozen.

I need your help, she said.

He followed her to a computer and she showed him a document. He noticed she was wearing her bonnet again.

Do you know how I can get in touch with these people, she asked.

It was a deed of sale to a house on South Mulberry Street.

Who do you want to get in touch with exactly, he asked.

The people who sold this house, she said.

Farber looked at the document closer.

It looks like the insurance company sold the house, he said. Was this a foreclosure?

I don't know, she said. Maybe. I don't know anything about this stuff.

Me either, he said. Looks here like it was sold to a property-management company.

He googled it and found their website.

Do you think I could use your phone, she asked.

You can use the one behind the front desk, he said.

She smiled again and Farber felt a sudden connection to her. The business with her changing clothes didn't seem as strange anymore. He wished he'd known her for a long time.

Do you mind watching my kid for a second, she asked.

Sure, he said. I can see her from the desk.

The child was sleeping in the big chair and she was wearing her bonnet again, too. The woman stood by the desk and dialed the numbers for the company.

Hi yes, she said. I'm calling about a property on South Mulberry that was recently sold. 241. Yes, exactly. I was wondering what happened to the former owner. Uh, huh. No, the owner before that. Oh. When? I see. OK, thank you.

She hung up the phone and sat down in front of the computer and started to do more searching. The hours melted by and Farber searched for new powers to give his avatar and watched cartoons on a tiny TV. Karen didn't buzz down to him all afternoon and without even noticing, it was almost five, an hour before closing. People began to wrap up their business. The woman came to the desk again and asked Farber if she could use his phone again.

Sure, he said. No problem.

He loved the way she stood and held the phone and wrapped the cord around her fingers.

Yes, hi, she said. I'm looking for one of your residents, Mrs. Miller. Yes. Right. Well, I'm her daughter. Uh, uh. Can you check again. OK. Can I talk to her? I see. OK. Thank you. I'll try again later. Goodbye.

She hung up.

Did you find what you were looking for, Farber asked.

I think so, she said. Thanks for all your help.

He realized they were alone. The library was peaceful and quiet. His favorite time of day.

So do you live around here, Farber asked.

I used to, she said.

Then she turned and paused.

Where's my baby, she asked.

What, he said.

My child, she said. Where is she?

Right over there, he said and pointed to the empty chair. Well, she was right there a minute ago.

I told you to watch her, she said.

I'm sorry, he said. She couldn't have gone far.

Carolina, she yelled. Carolina where are you?

2

AS SHE RAN THROUGH THE LIBRARY screaming for Carolina, Cleo thought of the night she left Harmony five years before. It was in the frantic days after the fire. Rain fell with Old Testament authority. Thick mud made some streets impassable but she drove on anyway despite the warnings on the radio that cautioned her in a weird robotic voice, breaking up the midnight classical station. She tried to smoke a cigarette but couldn't find a lighter. Water crept into the Jeep's canvas top and she could no longer see the road. As she made a turn before a bridge, she hydroplaned. The Jeep spun around three times and came to a sudden stop in a ditch just shy of the bridge. The headlights illuminated the violent winds up high in the dark magnolias. She was detached from the darkness for a moment and her heart gravitated toward a pure and intoxicating light. A death angel, she thought, until she remembered she didn't believe in such things.

Get away, she said to the light.

She was sure of the light, but couldn't decide its meaning or origin, only that her eyes were fading into it. Many hours passed but they were minutes to Cleo.

She remembered the light as she searched the library for Carolina. Through the history section and anthropology and life sciences. Carolina was always such an anxious girl, she thought. Even in the womb. Always struggling to get out. Almost clawing me to get free. Cleo thought of Caroline already growing inside her three weeks when the Jeep ran off the road that night five years before. She didn't know it then. It would be confirmed weeks later when she was already rescued. After the pickup truck found her, the bearded rain-soaked men and their dark silhouettes behind their flashlights, knocking on the Jeep as she woke. A tear of blood running down from her lips. They asked her if she was OK and she turned her head to see if she knew where she was and it was only the blinding light from the flashlights and the wet night behind it.

I don't know how I got here, she said.

As the men guided her, drenched and whimpering, into their old truck, and as they drove her past fallen trees and ruined houses, she realized she'd been driving straight into something terrible and if it wasn't for her tires giving out at that exact moment she would've been sucked away into oblivion. Many times in the years after she wished for exactly that. To have been swept away, but she wasn't, and she lived and the baby, the baby girl she named after her home state, lived too.

Carolina, Cleo screamed now throughout the library. She saw the guy in the fedora again. His mouth was slack and awful. He was like a thin version of a fat man. She'd pitied him when she was waiting outside but could see that in another life they could've been friends. She sensed in him a deep pain.

Carolina, she yelled. This isn't funny.

The guy in the fedora came to her.

I told you to watch her, she said.

She sat down and cried. She was struck back into the past. Time slipped away. Her life rewound until it stopped at the place when she came to believe in God. It was a slow process. Eventually her former feelings of doubt became a relic inside her. It was something about finding out she was with child. By then she had been on the compound with the bearded men and their women in bonnets for many months. They told her it was a sign and that it meant that she was destined to be among their chosen flock. For her, it was a functional thing. She couldn't have had the child by herself. She couldn't face her parents. So she thought why not pretend for a while.

The group that rescued her called themselves disciples of Christian naturalism and worshiped a Jeremiah Vanderlip who believed there were devils in your bloodstream and you should never wear red. They called themselves the Yellow Children of God. They gave Cleo clothes, long dresses. They had mountains of food each night, fresh from the farm. She had her own room overlooking the fields and woke each morning to the smell of dark coffee and bacon frying. There was little knowledge of the outside world, which was just fine with her. She didn't want to read about Iggy and the fire.

There was a school there but they didn't make her go. They

believed teens who were pregnant were closer to God. But after she had the baby, midwifed by an older woman, they made her a teacher at the nursery. One of the boys, he was almost twenty, with strong green eyes named Jamie stopped her one day on her way to work.

So you're our virgin mother, he said.

I'm not a virgin, Cleo said.

I was kidding, he said.

She smiled and he seemed to take her smile and imprison it. She fell in love with Jamie the same way she fell in love with Jesus, out of habit. Each morning at dawn she woke the children. She ate breakfast in the sun and was with children all day. She loved the children but wanted to be with someone her own age. Jamie was always there when she was done with her day. They all ate dinner at a long table. The whole fellowship.

Jesus is always with you, Jamie said on their first date.

Is that so, Cleo said.

But after a while, quite unexpectedly, she thought a lot about the idea of an all-knowing something out there. She felt that Jamie was worthy of her secrets and she told him about the night before the fire with Iggy, and how she'd been sleeping with Paul without Iggy knowing it. She was with Paul when he died. She couldn't bring herself to get rid of the baby. It was the only thing left of Paul.

Jamie gave her a hug.

I love you, he said. Jesus does, too.

Cleo married Jamie not long after that and they lived together in a house he built for her on a hillside. Late nights they stayed up talking, early mornings she walked the dog and he made the coffee. He always was gentle with Cleo and kind with Carolina.

Then one morning Jesus came to her on a walk. He spoke to hear as real as any man.

I'm not your father, Christ said. I am your brother.

Cleo stopped walking, unsure if she was hallucinating.

I will be with you along the way, Christ said. Look for me and you will find me.

She saw Jamie playing with Carolina in the grass and thought, If God gives him kindness then I'll believe in God. Then she said his name out loud.

Jesus, she said. I believe in you.

She told Jamie that night and he thanked her for being honest.

I knew you were doubtful, he said. Since the day I met you.

He kissed her.

There were months of bliss and they lived a life of freedom. Then one night he came to her.

I have something I want to tell you, he said.

He got up and shut the door. It was late and they had been drinking muscadine wine.

I hope you won't judge me, he said.

How bad can it be, she thought to herself. He is my husband. He has trusted me. I will stand by him no matter what.

I've been chosen to have another wife, he said.

Cleo sat in silence. She knew the elders had many wives, but it had never crossed her mind that Jamie would take another one.

Well you told them no, right, she asked.

Jamie shook his head.

This could be a really big deal for us, he said. No one gets a second wife at my age. I could be an elder in ten years.

It's because of Carolina, Cleo said. She's not your daughter.

No, Jamie said. You don't understand.

I don't think you do, Cleo said. I won't live like this.

What I say goes, he said. I'm the head of this household.

Later that night, after Jamie was asleep, Cleo went to Carolina's room and held her. She wrapped her in a sling around her breasts, climbed out the window, and walked down to the elders. She barged in on them drinking by the fire.

My baby is sick, she said. I need the truck.

You can't come in here like this, they said.

Cleo always hated the elders. They were old disgusting men who knew nothing of the world.

My baby is sick, she said again. I need the truck.

One of us will drive you, they said.

No, I need to do this on my own, she said. It's private. A lady's matter.

Where is your husband, they asked.

There was a knock at the door.

Haven't we had enough interruptions for one night, the elders said.

It was Jamie.

Deeply sorry, he said. I'll take care of this.

Very well, the elders said. Be gone.

That was the first night Jamie beat her with his belt. After he was finished, he felt sorry and tried to talk her out of leaving. Time moved like this in a cycle. Beatings and begging until she formed a plan. She waited for many weeks until he let his guard down. She and Carolina could sometimes ride to town with the elders when they went to the farmers market. Jamie had been wary, but that week he said it was OK. As soon as they arrived at the farmers market she ran to a policeman and demanded he take her back to Harmony. She was in trouble. The cop said there was nothing he could do. She'd have to make a report. Jamie beat her for two days straight for that episode. Then there was nothing for a month. No beatings. The days dragged on as they always did. They began to talk about his birthday. He told her he was saving up.

What do you mean, she asked.

You'll see, he said.

When the day came they had dinner, opened presents, sang Happy Birthday. Cut cake and put Carolina to bed then sat by the fire.

It's time for my present, he said.

We opened gifts already, she said.

My other present, he said.

He got out a picture.

This is Jacqueline, he said. She's from the settlement in Love Valley. She'll be joining us by Christmas.

How old is she, Cleo asked.

Fifteen, Jamie said.

I hate you, she screamed. I won't live with her.

Quiet, he said.

He punched her and she fell to the ground. Then he laid on top of her. She tried to kick him but he hit her again. With each blow, she got stronger. Every time he hit her she hit him back harder. He grabbed her by the throat. Darkness was closing but she kept hitting. She felt herself going limp but before she passed out a shaft of light fell on them. He stopped choking her. Carolina was at the door.

Go back to bed, Jamie screamed.

He moved toward Carolina.

Cleo jumped on his back and pulled his hair until he fell backward and hit his head on the hardwood.

She grabbed Carolina in one hand and a fire poker in the other. Without thinking, she went down hard toward his face. Deeply with each blow. She closed her eyes and hit until he fell to the ground begging her to stop. She ran out the door to the elders' house. They were playing cards. She knocked.

What, they said.

I need the truck, she said.

For what, they asked.

She saw the keys on the table, grabbed them, and ran out the door. They ran after her but she was too fast. She drove through the night to Harmony to her old house. It was empty. She slept in the truck bed with Carolina close to her. Nothing was open at that hour. She had no money and drove around until she saw the new library and parked in the lot and waited for it to open.

TRUDY HEARD THE COMMOTION in the library from the reading room upstairs. She went there in the afternoon because it was cool and quiet in the summer. Five years before they'd scattered Johnny's ashes into the Bluebird River, as he requested, so the library was the closest thing to a headstone. Trudy loved to get lost in some thick novel all alone up there and dream of Johnny.

After the fire she became a minor celebrity. Donation money began to pour in and she set up a foundation to build the new library. She also met a man. His name was Ringo P. Wilson, a highway patrolman. After the fire he was charged with protecting her. He sat in a patrol car for weeks outside her house. He was a thick, tall man. A former linebacker and captain in the Marines. After the fire there were death threats against Trudy's life. Some kind of conspiracy theory. People claimed she was a crisis actor.

I want you to stay close to me at all times, Ringo would say when they went anywhere.

She didn't mind being close to him. She loved how tight and clean his uniform was. How he made little jokes to her as they went to and from the car.

To Trudy, he felt like the men she used to date when she was a teenager, before she met her husband. Easy men, who knew what they wanted. It felt good to be held again. It happened one night as he brought her home from the store.

I'm off duty now, he said.

So, she said.

I thought maybe, he said. Maybe we could, you know, relax together.

You thought wrong, she said and went inside. A second later she came back out.

I'm just kidding, she said. Get in here.

He was gentle with her and they never left each other's side for the next four months. Spending their nights together drinking cheap wine and watching reality TV. They got married at the new Baptist church and honeymooned in Gatlinburg.

She often thought of how life was a paradox. She wished so much that Johnny and Ringo could have met. But if Johnny hadn't died she would've never had this happiness with Ringo.

She heard someone screaming downstairs.

Carolina, the voice shouted. Where are you?

The young woman screamed, her tan deep brown. Trudy walked downstairs. The girl was frantic. She touched her on the shoulder and stared into her eyes. Told her to take a deep breath.

I'm Trudy, she said. What's your name?

I'm Cleo, the girl said.

Cleo turned to her, recognizing her.

Do I know you, Cleo said.

I don't know, she said. I'm Trudy. Do you know me?

I can't find my daughter, Cleo said. Have you seen her?

Stay close to me, Trudy said. I know she's around here somewhere.

They walked through the stacks, each one, calling Carolina's name.

Farber joined them.

Ms. Trudy, Farber said. Karen said we have to call the police.

Nonsense, Trudy said. The little girl is around here, I'm sure. Children like to play hide-and-seek.

Then they heard crying. It was coming from the children's section. The bathtub. The three of them ran toward it and found Carolina curled up, crying to herself. She got out and instead of running to Cleo, she ran to Trudy. Her eyes full of tears.

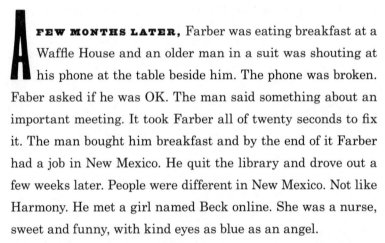

A **FEW MONTHS LATER,** Farber was eating breakfast at a Waffle House and an older man in a suit was shouting at his phone at the table beside him. The phone was broken. Faber asked if he was OK. The man said something about an important meeting. It took Farber all of twenty seconds to fix it. The man bought him breakfast and by the end of it Farber had a job in New Mexico. He quit the library and drove out a few weeks later. People were different in New Mexico. Not like Harmony. He met a girl named Beck online. She was a nurse, sweet and funny, with kind eyes as blue as an angel.

He lived in a large one-bedroom apartment on the outskirts of town and for the first time in his life, Farber didn't worry about where the rent was coming from. He worked as the man's personal computer guy and then was hired as the IT director of his company. The employees gave him access to their personal lives without even thinking. On dates he would tell Beck about some embarrassing detail he discovered on their computers.

This one guy is a furry, he said.

A what, she asked.

When he told her what it was she laughed for ten straight minutes. It was a big, joyous laugh. He could recognize it across a crowded room. Life was better in New Mexico, but he never forgot Harmony. As the weather turned cold he started to miss his hometown more and more, a place he never thought he would care about. That day at the library kept calling him. For a long time he couldn't even understand why that day had been so important. He couldn't describe it exactly. It was as if he could see inside these strangers' hearts. They had experienced something together. They'd found a lost girl, even if she wasn't far. The way they all stood out in front of the library as if they'd known each other forever. The light fell golden and warm around them and the air was charged with sweetness. Nothing terrible happened to them that day. He and the young mother, she told him her name was Cleo, stood together, the child still clinging to Trudy. They were all survivors of different storms washed up on the same shore.

After a date to the movies, Beck asked if she could come back to Farber's place. They made love. She didn't tell him it was her first time, and he didn't ask. He told her of his childhood surgery and she kissed his scar.

Does it hurt, she asked.

Not when you kiss me like that, he said.

She was the only person he allowed to know him fully, the only one who knew his secret pain. But there was more he wanted to say to her. He wanted to tell her about the library and the missing child that day and how they stood together as the sun died over the hills and it felt like they were a family, even if it was just for five minutes. The child had fallen asleep in Trudy's arms and she finally handed her back to Cleo. Love and pain weren't all that different, Farber thought. He realized he was capable of great sacrifice.

He tried to tell Beck all of this but it came out wrong.

There was a mother and a child and this other woman, he said.

He went on and on and finally gave up trying to tell the truth of it.

Beck kissed him. It was a long, slow kiss of new love.

Can we talk about it in the morning, she asked. I want to go again.

OK, he said.

She turned the lamp off. The room went dark.

CLOUD

2019

F IT WASN'T FOR THE VIETNAM WAR, she wouldn't have been born. Her father was a US Army captain. Her mother wore a wild rose in her hair, a waitress in a Hanoi cafe. They married and moved to America, settled in a little southern college town and named their only daughter Alabama. She looked like her mother and he talked with her father's southern drawl.

I'm Alabama, she said. Al for short.

I'm Joe McCloud, I said. Everybody calls me Cloud.

I met her when I was in college studying the poetry of John Milton. Al was a local, her father ran the law school. The town was the birthplace of a famous architect named Mary Hutton Hart, a genius of early modernism who despised her southern roots but the city fathers made her birthplace a museum anyway and the drugstore sold postcards of her face and every year a parade in her honor made its way through the square passing the clock tower that she designed. It stood silent after its bell broke decades before. They'd never raised enough money to make it toll the hour again like it did on old distant afternoons in the terrible years after the war. I saw Al for the first time one late autumn night drinking beer at the bowling alley, the only culture for miles. I couldn't resist her. Her movie-star eyes, biker boots, and ripped blue jeans. After a few hours, she asked me if I wanted to go skinny dipping at the motel pool at midnight and I said yes. We did bumps of cocaine off her car keys behind a dumpster and she touched my hips with her hands and pulled me close. We partied all night with her townie friends in an abandoned barn and later we made out in the bedroom of some rich man's house she knew was away on business. We ate sleeping pills so strong we slept through a storm. I was convinced the whole thing was a secret dream. The storm and the pills and motel pool and the barn and the rich man's house. All of it a dangerous fantasy.

Or maybe the storm wasn't the night we met. Maybe that night was dark and strange like so many other deep southern nights. We simply sat talking and drinking flat beer and the world was unexciting everywhere and the sky was calm over the broken clock tower whose bell didn't ring.

Life gets mixed up for me. Twisted and turned. My surest summer memories lose their leaves and the green yards of my recollections become white with fresh snow. What I do remember is one night we talked about the town and how we both wanted to move up north someday as she drove me in her Dad's muscle car down to the dry riverbed, her hot hand on my thigh, listening to Thin Lizzy.

You take these curves pretty fast, I said as we raced back to town along the country highway.

It's the only way I know how, she said.

We parked outside the last drive-in for a hundred miles and watched a soundless movie, Julia Roberts's huge face floating over the pines.

We should keep on driving and never come back, she said.

Where would we go, I asked.

To Mississippi, she said, New Orleans maybe or the good parts of Texas.

Then what, I asked.

She sat quiet as stone.

It was as if we were playing out some kind of lost teenage rebellion where pure freedom was only a matter of constant motion.

OK, I said. Take me somewhere. None of the old places. Somewhere fresh.

We drove over the border into Tennessee, maybe that was the night of the storm, and got a cheap hotel room and sat up drinking bedtime tea and smoking joints of shitty weed, exhaling through the bathroom fan. The TV in the room down the hall played Mexican talk shows all night full blast and we never said a word to each other. We made love, ordered a pizza, watched black-and-white westerns on mute and fell asleep to the rhythm of the rain. There was a simple dazzling honesty to the moment. What can I say about pleasure except that it is rare in this world without pain.

On the way back home, she told me she had to leave and go back to college in Virginia, she'd only taken the semester off to get her head straight. She said she wanted to keep in touch. She would be back for spring break. Maybe we could hang again.

Why didn't you tell me before all this, I asked.

Again she sat quiet as stone.

Or maybe she did say something, had some explanation, but I've already forgotten it along with a million other things that used to fill me with confidence. With a reality I used to know. Now sometimes it feels like I drift away each night into a warm fog and wake to find myself on a remote island.

After that I put Al out of my mind. Wrote my thesis on *Paradise Lost*. Spent the years after graduation working at the movie theater, writing bad poems about love gone rotten. I started dating Vicky, the projectionist, and after a year we moved in together. Sometimes those years come back to me like a sudden afternoon rain. Vicky was thin and tender with pink hair and a robot tattoo. She wanted something more than what the world had given her. Looking back, if I'm honest, I can't recall the feeling of a single day with her but instead remember her as a distinct sensation I can summon at will like the smell of sunflowers or the sounds of a county fair.

It'd been years since I'd even thought of Al when the bell began to ring on the clock tower. Vicky had gone to her parents' house in Biloxi for Christmas, we'd been fighting all week. I wasn't sure if she was coming back or if she did that we would last the month. I was working a late shift at the theater and walked out to my car on the square. In the distance I heard someone calling my name.

Al was running through the streets with a top hat on and a glass of champagne. She'd been at the wedding of the mayor's daughter.

The bell is ringing, she yelled. It's ringing again.

She was a vision from some alternate past. She spoke as though no time had come between us. As though we'd been in the middle of a conversation only minutes before.

Can you believe it, she said. They finally got it working.

I was so taken by the sight of her I hadn't noticed that the bell was, in fact, ringing. The shock of it brought people out of the bars and restaurants into the cold. Everyone enraptured by this ordinary, extraordinary sound.

Take me somewhere, Al said. We need to celebrate.

I unlocked my car.

You're drunk, I said. I'm going home.

Come on, she said. Don't do this to me. To Mary Hutton Hart's house. We must honor her.

Al got in the passenger's side.

No, I said. I can't do this.

Do what, she asked downing the rest of the champagne, throwing the empty glass in the backseat.

Whatever we're about to do, I said. We can't do it.

She took her top hat off and rolled down the window.

What are we about to do, she asked.

I don't know, I said. You tell me.

She produced a cigarette from behind her ear even though I'd never known her to smoke and she lit it with a wooden match like a general in an old war movie about to fight an un-winnable battle.

I'm tired, I said. How bout we get lunch tomorrow and catch up.

A van of partygoers rounded the square. Girls in expensive dresses, men in tuxedos with tails. They yelled for Al to join them. To get out of the car. The bell was ringing, they said. They were going to the river. Al shook her head and they drove away.

Can you forgive me, she said.

For what, I asked.

For leaving, she said.

I started the car.

The van was coming back around the square a second time.

Can we at least get out of here, she said. I want to be alone with you.

We drove toward Mary Hutton Hart's house and the sound of the bell faded a little. I parked away from the road and we got out and shared a cigarette on the hood of my car. It was an old British convertible I'd found in a junkyard and rebuilt. I never repainted it and loved its fading majesty.

She kissed me and I pushed her away.

Sorry, I said. I can't.

That's when she told me the story of how her parents met. How if it wasn't for some absurd war that killed hundreds of thousands, she wouldn't have been born. Every day she lived because someone else didn't. She was a product of misguided history and somehow all those decisions, big and little, had led us here to that freezing night. For many years I'd struggled to become a poet in that little town. Wringing out my misery in lines. I wanted to be known for something, singled out. It was strange but in that moment with Al telling me about her parents I decided I didn't want to become famous anymore. I wanted to fade into the nothingness of time, become a statistic and a stranger to the ages hence.

I'm freezing, I said.

Same, she said. But I don't want to go home.

We drove to the motel where we first went skinny-dipping all those years before and we got a room and undressed each other and took a long warm bath. I'm not sure what happened next. If we made love or drank beer or watched TV. Though I do remember that Al revealed to me her sins and I revealed mine but for the life of me I can't remember what they were. Instead, all my memory will allow is another mysterious night we shared together. I can't place it in time. My mind won't tell me if it was before all this or after but the image is striking. We were driving in the mountains late at night and the car broke down. It was 4:00 a.m. and we were lost and had no phone service. We decided to walk up the mountain to the nearest gas station ten miles away. After an hour or so a truck came by and an old couple was driving.

Need a lift, they asked.

We climbed in.

Why are you out so late, I asked.

There's a meteor shower, the wife said.

They took us down a dark country road to a sandstone outcrop overlooking the Blue Ridge. We lay on the rock. This old couple, Al, and me.

The wife said, Don't try to chase the shooting stars, instead find one fixed point in the heavens and let them come to you.

Soon the meteors burned through the sky. After a long pause, her husband spoke.

Like the blossoms of the falling cherry tree, he said.

This memory, the wife and her country zen husband, gets

mixed up with that night the bell began to ring again. I'm not sure why or what it means if it means anything at all but I think it has something to do with the way things come to an end. Soon after all this I got a call from Vicky. She was coming home. Then months went by and she was pregnant and then more months went by and she lost the child on a hot summer day. We made a little wooden cross on a hill overlooking the town and I never went back to that place.

The last time I saw Al was almost two years later. I'd moved to New Orleans. Got a job in an office making other people rich. One day on my lunch break I tried a new restaurant and Al was there waiting tables. She looked different. Her head shaved, fresh tattoos. When her shift was over we caught up. She smoked a cigarette out back while I sat on a milk crate. She told me she lived out west for a few years and her boyfriend had died in a car crash and she moved to the city. She was full of politics. Talked about joining black bloc soldiers fighting fascists in the streets. She was thinner than I remembered, but stronger, too. Her mystery had returned.

Revolution is a means of survival, she said. Money is like a living death.

I nodded because I didn't know what to say.

For Al, the intervening years had become heavy with the old tragedies of the world and some new ones, too. She smoked one cigarette after another. The afternoon was turning into evening, she was already drinking wine. Light haloed her head and I noticed she was missing a few back teeth. It was strange to see this person I had thought about so many lonely nights changed into a street mystic in black orthopedic shoes, ranting about guerrilla warfare and lovers dead on the Dakota blacktop.

That day at the restaurant reminded me of the second closest I ever came to dying. I was living at home with my aunt and uncle after college. Deeply depressed, I went out driving aimlessly with the intention of killing myself. In a fit of despair I intentionally ran a red light and almost hit a woman head on, but swerved at the last minute. I pulled over and turned the car off and watched the wind blowing through the trees like lungs inhaling and exhaling. It was like being banished from paradise into the world of life and death.

It was the first time in many years that I had thought of my mother. Memories of her are rare these days. I can recall even less about my father. Only what others have told me. I was four when they died. What I do remember are sensations. My mother's cold hands on my forehead, checking for a temperature. My father's crisp work coats hanging in his closet. I thought about the day the chaplain came and told me they were going to finally execute Iggy. I was away at church camp. He told me after chapel near a big magnolia tree.

We got word his appeals failed, he said. Tonight at midnight, he'll be dead.

I sat up all night checking the clock listening to my roommate snore. I almost fell asleep a few times but kept myself awake. I wanted to see the clock strike midnight. I wanted to know when he was dead. I watched the minutes tick by. Finally when the hour struck midnight, an enormous relief came over me. It was as if I had been carrying a great weight for a long distance without knowing it. I thought of my mother. The sound of her voice calling me in for supper. The way she would laugh on the phone for hours to my aunt.

As I fell asleep that night I thought about living in Mississippi with my aunt and uncle. They raised me in the hill country after the fire. One night, I must've been about fifteen, they were up drinking, watching TV. Out of nowhere a violent storm began outside. We went to the porch and everything was raging and black. The heavens opened and it began to hail. My aunt grabbed me and took me inside. We huddled in a closet. The lights went out. It sounded like a freight train outside. Then, as quick as it came, the storm was gone. My uncle got out the flashlights and we went outside. The ground was covered in ice. White globes the size of tennis balls covered the yard. The night was clear and a full blue moon reflected in them as if a million tiny moons had landed in the grass.

We started to hear footsteps crunching in the ice. In the distance was a young woman walking down the street. Blood was streaming down her face. She was out of a horror movie with the light from my uncle's flashlight in her face.

Hey, I said. What are you doing out here?

My car, she said. I ran off the road.

Get out of the street, my uncle said. Power line's down.

She was tall and thin. The same age as my mother when she died. Her hair was brown and long, the way some country girls still keep it.

I was working the late shift, she said. Couldn't get home before the storm.

Let's get inside, my uncle said. We'll call someone.

She came inside and my aunt got her a towel and something warm from the laundry room. One of my flannel shirts. Two sizes too big. She called a friend to pick her up, but the roads were closed. They were going to be a little while.

Have a beer while you wait, my uncle said. Gotta drink them or they'll get hot.

She doesn't want a beer, my aunt said.

No, the woman said. I'll drink one.

My name's Maggie, she said.

I'm Joe, I said. Friends call me Cloud.

We played cards all night under candlelight, Maggie was on my team. We won every time. My aunt and uncle got drunk and started telling stories on each other. It was the first time I'd ever felt close to them. Mostly we watched TV in silence, but that night I felt like a family. At one point my uncle was bringing back beers from the kitchen and had an extra. He slid it my way.

It's time, he said.

Really, I said.

Yeah, he said. You've earned it.

He's too young, my aunt said.

He deserves it, Maggie said. He saved me.

The beer tasted awful but I drank every drop. I wanted to impress this stranger. We played more games: go fish, poker, gin. It was almost 3:00 a.m. before the lights were back on. The stereo came alive full blast playing Sly and the Family Stone. We all jumped up. Started dancing we were so excited. Maggie took me by the hands and I dipped her as I'd seen in movies. Everyone thought that was so funny. This kid and this woman, dancing. They laughed and laughed. Then it was time for her to go.

The last thing I remember was what Maggie said at the end of the night. Her ride was there and she was saying thank you to my aunt and uncle. She tried to give my flannel back but I said she could keep it.

You've raised such a fine boy, she said.

I was tipsy. I didn't want her to go.

They're not my parents, I said. My parents are dead.

My aunt and uncle looked at each other. Maggie's ride honked outside. She walked over to me and kissed me on the forehead.

You're one of the good ones, she whispered.

I swear it was the voice of my mother.

I read somewhere that the earth only has a couple of good years left. Soon it'll be too hot to live. I assume I'll end before the world does, my mind already fading toward oblivion. Some days are better than others but when things are bad I'm like a child that believes if they close their eyes the world will disappear. I'll be dust soon and they'll put a gravestone over me and in time that too will turn to dust and nothing will exist. Before that happens I wanted to put down in writing some things that I've loved and remind you that, for now, I persist. My little dog is scared of thunder. I drink tea and read the paper in the evening. When I put tulips in the window, they open toward the sun. Someone in the distance is calling my name.

A NOTE ABOUT THE AUTHOR

Michael Bible is the author of *Sophia* and *Empire of Light*. Originally from North Carolina, he lives in New York City.

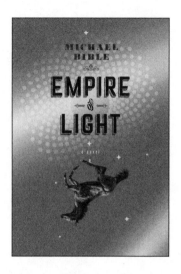

"Bible roots out the sublime pleasures available
at the searing edge of depressed feeling.
Denis Johnson seems to be the abiding spirit of the
novel, which achieves the incendiary strangeness
of his prose . . . Bible offers us a remarkable
vision of adolescence as not just a time of extreme
exposure but one of visionary longing."
—*The New York Times*

"A shorthand masterpiece of style, a
tour de force of voice."
—Tom Franklin, author of *Crooked Letter, Crooked Letter*

"*Empire of Light* is a truly beautiful book."
—William Boyle, author of *Gravesend*

"A euphoric, one-of-a-kind novel."
—*Arkansas International*